ALL OVER THE NEWSPAPERS. . . .

I felt numb. In some ways she'd been my best friend. But I had to pull myself together. The police would probably be showing up soon. My name was in her LeFax on the murder day.

Alex was sitting in the client comfy chair with his feet on my desk. His hands made a temple. He said, "What are you doing?"

I took off my skirt, jacket, and blouse. In times of crisis, wearing a skirt makes me feel out of control. I had a pair of 501s in the bottom drawer of my desk. Also there's a Benetton sweater, fresh undies, a box of tampons, a bottle of Amaretto for clients, a spritzer of Love's Baby Soft and a blow-drier. You never know when you'll get caught in the rain. I didn't care too much if Alex saw me in my bra and undies. His eyes widened.

He said, "You're naked. Right in front of me. Somehow I'm seeing things in a whole new light."

I said, "I'm not in the mood for trading metaphors." I brushed lint off my 501s and slipped them on. I felt the difference instantly. In control. No way could I handle greeting the police in a mini. . . .

A DEADLINE FOR MURDER

VALERIE FRANKEL

POCKET BOOKS
New York London Toronto Sydney Tokyo Singapore

This book is a work of fiction. Names, characters, places and incidents are either the product of the author's imagination or are used fictitiously. Any resemblance to actual events or locales or persons, living or dead, is entirely coincidental.

An *Original* Publication of POCKET BOOKS

POCKET BOOKS, a division of Simon & Schuster
1230 Avenue of the Americas, New York, NY 10020

ISBN: 0-671-73021-5

First Pocket Books printing February 1991

10 9 8 7 6 5 4 3 2 1

POCKET and colophon are registered trademarks of Simon & Schuster.

Printed in the U.S.A.

Dedicated to Howie, Judy, Al, and Jon.
Thanks for the atmosphere—
and ten books' worth of dialogue.

Special thanks to: Leslie Wells, for knowing how much was too much; Loretta Fidel, for taking a chance; Marilyn Johnson, for generosity and guidance throughout; Stacy Title, for hooking me up; Judy McGuire, for giving me work when I was broke; and Joel Tractenberg, for letting me test his patience every single day during the writing of this book.

CHAPTER ONE

WHAT HAVE I DONE TO DESERVE THIS?

Double margarita afternoon at Harry's Muncheteria with Belle. That's what she told me to write in my book for Monday, October 15, when we made plans. I was sick of Harry's, but she insisted we hit our usual spot. Belle always gets her way.

"You feel that yet?" Sal, waiter extraordinaire and all-around dreamy guy, asked, pointing at my drink.

"Not as much as I'd like to," I said.

"Well, I'm just loopy," Belle said. Sal turned to walk away. Belle called him back. "Excuse me, Sal, dear. I just wanted to tell you what a fine job you're doing today. The drinks couldn't be tastier." Belle giggled in her stylishly slutty way. "You're looking sweet today, Sal. I'm loving your adorable set of lips. Nice mouth, don't you think, Wanda? Simply luscious. Here's to your bottom lip, and to all the lucky women who get to suck it." Belle took a slug. "Skoal."

It's been a while for Belle. Must be up to a few hours by now.

The midtown lunchers crammed into Harry's, escaping the hammering and banging of the endless construction of 44th Street. All the tables were littered with burned fries, beer buckets, and full ashtrays. Life in the smoking section. Men aimed furtive darts at our table. I couldn't tell if they were for me or for Belle. As a dozen more blue suits crushed their way into the joint Sal returned. He placed a shot of tequila in the middle of my plate and curled his ever so adorable mouth. Belle said, "Sal, is that on the house? Is that for her? What about me?"

Sal, the stoic, said, "You're doing fine already."

What can I say? Waiters like me. Taxi drivers even more.

Belle drank my shot. She properly dabbed her mouth and said, "Do you emit some kind of weird hormone or something? What is it—the tits? Christ, you're not even pretty." She bit down on the lime. She said, "It's not that you're not attractive. You do have that bestial sexual appeal that excites plebes like Sal. You're just not gorgeous. You know what I mean. In this city, it takes gorgeous." She exhaled loudly and shook a loose blond strand from her forehead.

Have I mentioned that Belle is gorgeous? She's got the whole look: straight blond hair pinned back at the base of her skull exhibiting cheekbones you could slice bread with. Belle slinks when she walks—straight from the Joan Crawford fuck-me school—even on line at the bank. She's slim—her bane. She longs to be skinny. She stays in shape swimming three times a week at the Health and Racket Club. No tits, though, as she often complains. I have no great affection for my tits either. But for the opposite reason.

I said, "Look, Belle, not that I don't appreciate your appraisal of my physical abnormalities—really, you've been wonderfully enlightening—but I've got to get back to the office soon." I have my own agency, Do It Right Detectives. I carry a gun—a pearl-handled .22. Not much more than a BB gun, but big men have been killed with smaller bullets. Belle calls it a whimsical accessory. I call it Mama.

She said, "The gun-toting gumshoe off on a case. How titillating."

"Your case," I replied. Belle is a client, and someone in need of friends. She comes in with a new pursuit every month or so, usually wanting me to trail her latest obsession. This month, his name is Johann—a Swede with a dick as long as his hair. To say he was attractive would be an insult. I said, "I've got some info for you."

She said, "Do you. How long have you been on this case, three weeks? Typical, Wanda." Belle spun her Chanel charm bracelet. She said, "You and deadlines have never been good friends. Especially when you worked at my magazine. Maybe you should have gotten a job as a full-time procrastinator instead of a detective."

"I get the job done."

"Diligence, Wanda dear, is the key to success."

"Your man Johann is into some kinky shit," I said.

"Philip Roth kinky, or Henry Miller?"

"Charles Bukowski."

"I find that hard to believe."

I said, "Maybe you don't know him so well."

"He proposed to me last night. I said yes. Anything that could upset my complacency might not be entirely welcomed." Belle lowered her peepers and chased a lime rind around her plate with a fork.

I said, "Complacency doesn't mean squat if you can't see past your tits. Which in your case isn't too far."

She said, "Must you be so vulgar?"

The problem with discussing Belle's life of debauchery is that I never make it back to the office without chaperoning her teary trip to the ladies' room. Sure, she's as tough as any self-made woman, but all marshmallow inside. She dropped her fork in her plate and plunked her head in her hands, an elbow nearly tipping her third margarita. Belle's sign: Help wanted.

I always get suckered into feeling sorry for her during times like this. I said, "Belle, come on. It's okay. Please, don't cry. You know I hate to see you cry."

She said, "That's what Johann said to me last night." Shit. That opened the floodgates. Belle told me once that as a woman in her position (which is usually prone), she can do whatever the fuck she wants. Which includes fucking whatever and whomever she wants. I'll never understand how she manages to stay so successful considering her emotional tidal waves. How she got so successful—well, that's another story.

Belle planted her nose between thumb and forefinger, nearly dipping her sleeve in ketchup. She didn't seem receptive to a moment of quiet consolation at our table. She made the noise: a soulful outgushing of air, reminiscent of the humpback whale's song I'd heard on channel 13. The rerun from so many of our past lunches followed. I took her by the elbow and led her to the bathroom. Hysterical, chicly dressed women who make ten times what I do are not my idea of a rollicking good time. Especially Belle. It's hard for me to see her this way since most of the time (when she doesn't act like Queen Hormone) I'm actually a big fan of hers. But, for fear of having to pay the bill, I had to help her out. I maneuvered her into our porcelain-and-tile sanctuary, and she unfolded across the long sink.

She sniffled. She sobbed. She breathed deeply. I thought she'd pass out. I tilted my head sympathetically and wound down some brown fit-for-the-litter-box paper towels. I gingerly placed them next to her writhing body. Melodrama à la Belle. It stopped being amusing after the hundredth time. I sat on one of the johns, placing my bag by the door to prop it open, lit a cigarette, fondled Mama to relax me, and waited for details.

She said, "He's just too much for me."

I said, "Tell me what happened, Belle."

She said, "He went down on me for hours."

I said, "For hours?"

She said, "Hours, damn it. Fucking hours. He wouldn't stop, even when I wanted him to. He made me come so many times—I felt like an epileptic." She spasmed a bit for demo. "I don't think I look too attractive while I'm coming. Silly, I know. How could I not look attractive?"

I'll give her that. Even with lipstick halfway up her nose and black lines running down her cheeks, she looked great. She said, "He fucked me like he was stealing home. I was closer to death than I've ever been last night. He taught me more about sex than any Greenwich girl should ever know. And I loved it. I loved him. And I told him. I told him that I loved him." Spasm, writhe. Humpback whale impression.

I said, "What did he say?"

She said, "He told me he loved me, too."

I said, "So, what's the problem?" I was hedging. After what I'd found out about the Swede, I didn't think it possible.

She said, "I only said it because I didn't know how to stop him."

"Stop him from what?" I asked.

"From hurting me."

I said, "Hurting you how? Physically? S & M?"

"I can't really go into it right now." Belle looked genuinely scared for a second, then shook it off. She hopped off the sink and stood in front of the mirror. She said, "It's part of our love."

She glanced quickly at my reflection in the bottom left corner. She said, "Give me a drag."

I got up off my seat and gave her my cigarette. She inhaled deeply and said, "So, what did you find out?"

I said, "You're not going to like it."

"Try me. I like almost anything these days."

I said, "These days?" I smiled at her.

"You don't know nearly as much about me as you think you do, Wanda. There are times when I'm just an old-fashioned girl." Belle cranked down another paper towel and touched up her face.

I said, "Okay. Brace yourself. Your man Johann isn't what old-fashioned girls call marriage material."

"That's a dubious distinction anyway." Belle yanked a hairbrush from her Chanel bag. I liked her black Hermès purse better, but she'd lost it recently—

unusual for Belle to misplace such a pricey item, I'd thought when she mentioned it.

I said, "He dallies. With other women." Belle didn't even twitch. I figured she already knew.

"I don't believe it. Not this time."

I said, "Believe it."

She'd taken out her hair clip and methodically stroked the brush through her hair. "No, he loves me too much. And it's not like you haven't been wrong before." She was talking about my investigation of a married man she was seeing a year ago. I told her he'd spent the whole day at City Hall getting a divorce. It turned out to be his twin brother. So sue me.

"I'm getting a little tired defending myself for one tiny mistake I made a year ago. I haven't been wrong since—you know that. Besides, I've got proof."

She said, "I'm waiting." And she was applying fresh lipstick.

"Did Johann bring you any presents last night?"

"Flowers. He always brings fresh daffodils."

I said, "He didn't give you a special love toy?"

"What are you talking about?" she asked.

"You and Johann ever play games?"

Belle jammed her brush back in her purse. She turned to me and said, "What is your point, Wanda?"

"I followed Johann into the Snack Happy bondage shop. He got two pairs of handcuffs and a penis-handled feather duster. He told the salesgirl that his girlfriend also wanted some vibrating eggs."

She looked into the mirror. She said, "What makes you so sure he wasn't buying that stuff for me?"

I said, "If he did, then I apologize. But did he?" I knew he didn't; I could tell from her expression.

She didn't answer for a few seconds. Then she said, "I wonder too often these days why I keep you on. You're always coming up with these meaningless, dreadful snippets. I'm not saying that I believe in any magical Mr. Right nonsense. But you make me feel like I have some kind of homing signal that attracts all the lying, cheating men in this stinking city. You're a doomsayer. And too much of a reminder of how few good men there are left. I think I've had enough disappointments with you. I think it's time for us to stop doing this."

I said, "So you're firing me because I do a good job."

"If you want to see it that way." She'd become totally cold. Businesslike.

I said, "You must really like this guy."

"That has nothing to do with our situation."

"You're letting your hormones define whom you want to spend time with."

She said, "We can still spend time together. I just won't pay you anymore."

I said, "So then you let your hormones define who's on your payroll. And don't try to convince me you aren't giving Johann any money." She slapped me. Hard. I almost felt I deserved it. She ran out into the dining room.

I chased after her. I said, "Belle, I'm sorry. I'm just doing my job."

She shrieked venomously, "Your services are no longer required. You'll have to find some other rich woman to support you." The blue suits at the next table kept a poker face. Sal came over to help. Belle threw a fifty in his face and said, "I can buy better lays than some waiter like you." The entire restaurant kept a poker face.

On that, hell's fury stormed out of Harry's, leaving me to caress Mama. I let it sink in that I might have lost more than my best client. I resolved to call her later and try to patch things up. My plan changed, however, when I read the newspapers the next morning.

I was in my Times Square office, and Alex Beaudine, my friend and colleague, walked in with two double espressos. I only drink coffee when I want to feel extra-specially confident: normally, my stomach won't tolerate it. I figure if I can down the caffeine, then I can take anything. It's a private torture test, and Alex must have known I was up for the challenge that morning. He handed me a cup, sat down across from me, put his feet up on my desk, and said, "It doesn't look like a good morning for you." He coughed, then said, "Nice outfit."

Alex works at Do It Right part-time. He's a photographer and is busy putting together his portfolio for an NEA grant. Alex and I share a blithe irreverence toward what we call reality. We are also both twenty-seven. Our physical similarities stop at age; where I'm soft and buxom, he's lithe and toned. My hair is a red curly mess, and his is straight and dark. I've got sharp green eyes, his are a lucid brown. I suppose Alex is attractive; having to describe him this way forces the issue, but I don't think about him like that. For one thing, we work together; also, I think he has a girlfriend. I haven't met her yet, but I've met a few of his old ones. They tend to wear a lot of pink. So, I must not be Alex's type anyway. He likes to dress in 501s, white Converse high-tops, and T-shirts, regardless of the season or situation. And he is always impeccably well-shaven. Another difference between us.

My office is clean, a happy relief for clients when they come in from the slime and grime of 42nd Street. Alex keeps the place immaculate. I'm not a candidate for godliness myself. My fixations tend to be more oral. There are two views from the windows: one of the news zipper in Times Square, the other of a hideously tacky hotel on 45th Street. The rest of the office is pretty low class. I've got a desk (wood, thank God—one leg wobbly), a few chairs (one comfy for clients, and a straightback behind my desk that's a few inches too short—I usually sit on a case file), a torch lamp, a coat rack, a desk clock, a file cabinet, and several heaping ashtrays. One is a standing ashtray like the ones you see in 1950s movies. To go with that, I found a table lighter at an antiques junkyard on Atlantic Avenue in Brooklyn. I keep that on my desk. Oh, I do have a carpet. It's as subdued as orange can be—it came with the space. Rent is due in two weeks. Not to mention my credit card bills.

If I lost Belle, my star client, Do It Right would be irreparably damaged. After my lunch with her I'd jogged back to the office and pored over my bills after telling Alex the whole story. Belle's Johann coverage was all we've had for weeks; her pocket change paid my rent. Without her, and with no new prospects, we'd be broke in a matter of days. I'd slumped home to Brooklyn and with Otis, my strapping young she-cat by my side, I'd devised a strategy to lure her back.

Belle is the consummate manipulator. The scary thing was that she was also incredibly volatile. I had to get her before she found some other private dick. I was prepared to grovel, not entirely losing my self-respect, but with adequate pathos. If Belle has one fatal flaw, it is her love of flattery.

I'd call on her at the magazine. Have I mentioned that Belle is an editor? She launched *Midnight* magazine, soft-core erotica "For Single and Married Women." Mainly literature, a few Vaseline-lensed shots—nothing too raunchy. Belle has a good reputation. Everyone accepts that she's brilliant, even her male counterparts at other skin rags. I got to know Belle when I worked at *Midnight* as a reporter/fact-checker, before I left to sleuth. As with most reporters, it was a longtime fantasy of mine. My first field job was with the Binkerton P.I. agency. I worked there for a few months. When my art-collector grandmother died, leaving me a Picasso ink sketch worth a few grand, I took that money and started Do It Right with Alex. But that's another story.

I planned to arrive at *Midnight* first thing. She'd see me, I knew that. Sure, she'd make me wait, probably an hour or so. They were busy with the annual Anaïs Nin celebratory issue. Belle herself was editing an essay on the ultimate eroticism of sex during menstruation. But however swamped, Belle's always got another mouthful to spit out. I'd let her give it to me, then I'd move in. I decided to wear a magaziney Azzedine Alaïa suit of black and purple. Miniskirt, long jacket, white blouse with big buttons, and black sheer stockings. I'd wear my Joan & David heels. I'd sit decorously and remorsefully. I'd wait for her to finish telling me off. Then I'd play her the same way I did a year ago, during the aftermath of the married man incident. I would gush, she would scowl; I'd gush some more, she'd give in.

I came back to the present when Alex said over his espresso, "Drink up. You've got to get your butt over to *Midnight.* Time's a-wasting."

I said, "You're right. Wish me luck." I quickly downed the remaining espresso, burning my tongue slightly. Alex stood when I did. He came over to me to inspect my outfit. He asked me to turn for a full view. He nodded in silence and gave me a low whistle. He put his hands on my shoulders and looked down at my face.

He said in a peculiarly serious voice, "Wanda, no matter what happens, you'll be okay. Other people out there love you."

I said, "My parents love me."

He said, "Yeah, well, I happen to think you're pretty great, too."

I looked hard at him. I said, "What is this? Are you making fun of me?"

"Take it however you want it."

"Alex, are you revealing a latent emotional fixation on me?" He grinned. I said, "Not today, dear. I have a headache."

"Don't flatter yourself, Wanda. And your slip is showing." He pointed at my leg.

I said, "You cad. The way you toy with my feelings." Alex and I fool around like this often. It's all completely harmless. Like I said, he's got something going—they could be engaged for all I know. He's a pretty private guy when it comes to his personal life.

"All I said was that I think you're great. Why is it so difficult for you to swallow niceness?"

I said, "I'm not wearing a slip." Alex flopped his brown hair over one eye, which, I must say, is incredibly charming. He handed me my coat, patted me on the butt, and shoved me out the door.

My first stop on my first outing of the day is always at the corner newsstand. I don't know the name of my newsstand man. I'd guess it's Abdul or Ahmed. I know this bucks the trend of most television shows, but I don't get the feeling that my stand man wants to offer his name. He's just fine with calling me pretty, and my calling him hey, you. I'm nearsighted, and I had left my glasses at the office, so I couldn't see the headlines on the papers until I was standing right in front of them.

When I got close enough to read the front pages I got that sick feeling, a real down-the-gullet queasiness that comes only with death. They said: SEX MAG HEAD FOUND DEAD and PORN QUEEN'S LAST STAND. A closer look confirmed that Belle was dead. I bought the *Daily Mirror* and clicked back to the office in my Joan & Davids.

Alex said, "That was quick."

I felt numb. In some ways she'd been my best friend. But I had to pull myself together. I said, "We are in deep shit. I mean deep. Deeper than those blind fish who live in caves on the bottom of the ocean. As deep as deep can be." (I'd learned about the fish in *National Geographic.)* I threw my coat across the room and knocked over the upright ashtray. Alex hadn't emptied it while I was gone. Cigarette butts scattered over the orange carpet.

He looked concerned. He said, "What the hell is wrong with you? I just vacuumed." I plopped down behind my desk and frantically flipped open to the Belle coverage. Alex watched me. He said, "This is for real, isn't it? What happened?" God, I thought, the police would probably be showing up soon. My name was in her LeFax on the murder day.

I said, "Look, Alex, we've got to get our shit together before the police get here."

Alex shouted, "The police? What the fuck is going on?"

"Read this," I said, throwing the papers at him.

Alex read the story from the *Daily Mirror* out loud. It said the following:

> Editor of pornographic *Midnight* magazine, Belle Beatrice, 35, was strangled to death in her Central Park West apartment late last night. According to police on the scene, her home was completely in order, ruling out the possibility that the prominent magazine editor fought to thwart a bungled robbery attempt. In fact, says a police officer, Ms. Beatrice had no other visible scars or wounds. It is possible, he said, she was throttled so efficiently that she was unable to fight with her attacker for her life.
>
> Her body was found by her alleged fiancé,

Swedish national Johann Pesto, at 3:00 A.M. Mr. Pesto says he telephoned the police immediately upon finding the body. Paramedics arrived and drove Ms. Beatrice to Saint Barnabas. A fruitless attempt to resuscitate her was made; however, she was pronounced dead on arrival by emergency room physicians. The coroner on duty estimated the time of death to be between the hours of 10:00 P.M. and midnight last night.

Mr. Pesto spent the night at Precinct 12 for questioning. He stated that he'd planned to marry the notoriously free-wheeling Beatrice. "I can't expect you people to understand our love," he said tearfully to reporters outside the precinct, "but we were devoted to each other." Beatrice's grieving parents, Anne and Bradley Beatrice of Greenwich, Connecticut, were called by detectives to confirm Pesto's claims. The Beatrices said they knew nothing of him or of their daughter's plans to marry. Further investigation of Pesto will follow.

Readers of *Midnight* magazine will sorely miss the late editor, who has twice won the American Society of Magazine Editors award for general excellence, as will her colleagues at the magazine. "I don't know what we'll do without her," says Herb Stoltz, managing editor. "She embodied the magazine. She was its spirit and heart." The editors at *Midnight* are planning a special issue to commemorate its founder in upcoming months. See obituary in this afternoon's *Mirror.*

* * *

Alex said, "Strangled. Not the way I'd want to go."

I was stockingless behind my desk. I said, "Let me think for a second." I thought about the police.

Alex said, "Too bad it had to be Belle. I was just starting to like her."

I said, "The police are coming to question me about the murder of Belle Beatrice." I thought about the agency.

Alex said, reading my mind, "You know something, Wanda? Without Belle, Do It Right could go under."

"I'm aware of that, Alex," I said. Under my breath: "Think about the agency."

Alex said, "What?"

"Think about the agency."

"I am thinking about the agency."

I said, "I wasn't talking to you, idiot. I was talking to myself."

Alex said, "You should be thinking about Belle."

Don't think about her.

I said, "I have to concentrate on Do It Right now, if you don't mind. How are we going to survive this? We can't very well get Johann as a client. Freelance for the police? Never. Bounty hunters? Have you got that in you?" I stood and started to take off my suit. I was dying to change.

Alex was sitting in the client comfy chair with his feet on my desk. His hands made a temple. He said, "What are you doing?"

I took off my skirt, jacket, and blouse. In times of crisis, wearing a skirt makes me feel out of control. I had a pair of 501s in the bottom drawer of my desk. Also there's a Benetton sweater, fresh undies, white Vans, a box of tampons, a bottle of Amaretto for clients, a spritzer of Love's Baby Soft, and a blow-drier. You never know when you'll get caught in the rain. I didn't care too much if Alex saw me in my bra and undies. His eyes widened.

He said, "You're naked. Right in front of me. Somehow I'm seeing things in a whole new light."

I said, "I'm not in the mood for trading metaphors." I brushed lint off my 501s and slipped them on. I felt the difference instantly. In control. No way could I handle greeting the police in a mini.

He said, "I hadn't realized how attractive you are until now."

I said, "Get serious for five minutes, please. I've got to piss."

I walked to the bathroom down the hall in my bra and jeans (the other offices on our floor are vacant). By the time I got back Alex was behind my desk picking pills off my Benetton. I said, "Hand me that spritzer. In the drawer. Come on." He dug around too long to find my Love's. Leaning across my desk in the transfer, he knocked the newspapers on the carpet and bent down to pick them up. He was beginning to annoy me.

He smiled and said, "I guess I'm just another guy who can't do anything right."

I said, "No, you're just another guy who has the sensitivity of a firing squad. Belle was strangled. The police are within minutes of breaking our door down. My entire life may be canceled due to lack of funds. And I'm not interested in playing your little flirt games right now. This is all clear, right? I'm not going too fast for you, am I?"

"Belle's murder sure has turned you into a bitch."

So I can be a bitch. That only came with the

territory. I traded in one life for the life of a hardboiled detective. A private dick. Chasing people in cabs, looking through windows with binoculars. Talking to doormen. Well, maybe that doesn't sound so hardboiled. But if not in action, I am in attitude. But I don't think feeling a bit jumpy when an old friend gets killed is cause for alarm.

I said, "If you can't take it, why don't you get the hell out? And don't forget to gas up my broom before you go."

"I don't want to leave you alone. You're obviously upset."

"I'm under control."

"You always are," he said.

"You say that like you're accusing me of something." I grabbed the spritzer from his hands and sprayed. A nipple popped out of my bra.

We heard two raps on the door. I yelled, "Get lost." The door opened.

One said, "Isn't this sweet."

The other said, "You've been expecting us, I see."

What they saw: my half-undressed profile, squirting a blast of Love's Baby Soft under my arm. I turned to face them. What they saw: my right nipple. At least, that's all they were looking at—like deer hypnotized by high beams. I adjusted my bra, pulled on my sweater, and sat behind my desk. I picked up my bag, touched Mama for luck, found a cigarette, and lit it. I took a deep breath and said, "If it isn't my two favorite public dicks."

Detective Dick O'Flanahey, dark and burly with a Simon Legree mustache, spoke first. "You know, sweetie, I don't respect you anymore, having seen you nekkid." He moved closer. "But I like you better." I blew smoke in his face, and he smiled. Cops like him never take women seriously, which is about as comforting as sandpaper underwear.

I smiled. "Public dick Dick. What tears you from the trough?"

Dick smiled and said, "You're a smart one, aren't you, sweetie?"

Alex was standing behind my desk next to me. He said, "Wanda, aren't you going to introduce me to your friends?"

"Alex Beaudine, meet detectives Dick O'Flanahey and Tom Squirely. Homicide." Everyone nodded in that noncommittal boy way.

Alex said, "A social call, I trust?"

They ignored him. Detective Tom "Bucky" Squirely, who could have been cute if he didn't have such buck teeth, said, "Mallory, we've come to take you downtown."

"You can't arrest me! All I did was have lunch with the lady. She was my client. That can't make me a suspect." My mind was racing.

Bucky whipped out his notebook and said, "Do you know Sal Marrone?"

"Waiter at Harry's. So he told you we got in a little tiff. Big deal. Belle was in hysterics constantly. You could get Sal to tell you a hundred stories."

Dick said, "All about you, cupcake."

I said, "And I thought he liked me." Cross waiters off my list.

Dick came even closer and said, "Sal does like you. You're the only one he remembers."

Bucky laughed uncontrollably. He sucked in air

with incredible force and said, "Come on, Dick. Let me be the bad cop once in a while. I always play the good cop."

I said, "You both stink, if you ask me." Private dick vs. cop. The age-old conflict. I hadn't always felt so antagonistic toward policemen. When I was younger, skipping around the Short Hills Mall was, for me, an eight-year-old's answer to sex. I would run from store to store, popping candy and cookies from my regular shopkeeper victims. I would usually lose my mother in a matter of minutes. But that never worried me. There were always two cops planted on the second floor, right by Sbarro's. I'd skip on over in that carefree little rich-kid way, flirt with the cops (yes, flirt—the way eight-year-olds will), and wait for Mom to come find me. She probably liked having the time alone. It must have improved the quality of her shopping. She'd say to the young officers, "Thanks for watching little Wanda for me." They'd say, "Our pleasure," and I'd squirm with delight. I thought there was an understanding between me and the men in blue. They lusted for me, I teased them mercilessly. That was the game. My mom probably thought when I grew up I'd have some kind of weird sexual obsession with men in uniforms, and I suppose I do. I hate them.

Dick said, "Okay, Tom. You be the bad cop. I've got to take a piss." On that, he lumbered off down the hall.

These two are especially loathsome. They have a reputation among the P.I.s in New York. Dick and Bucky have two hobbies: harassing private dicks and harassing each other. Theirs is the classic sadomasochistic relationship. I've come across them twice before. And both times I succumbed—which means I gave them the information they needed. I figured they wanted information on Johann. I had a file big as an area phone book on him, complete with oodles of savory detailia. This time I resolved to stand my ground. They'd never see that file.

Alex said, "Now that we've covered the histrionics, maybe we can get to the point. Wanda had nothing to do with Belle's death."

Bucky said to Alex, "And you've got nothing to do with this investigation." Bucky turned to me and said, "You're not in good shape, Mallory. We have witnesses that will testify about your argument with Belle. We also have a source that claims Belle was your primary source of income. Maybe you tracked her down and asked her to hire you back. Maybe she refused. Maybe you went crazy. Maybe you strangled her." Bucky paused. His squinty eyes bore into defiant ones. Melodrama is like a disease in this city.

I said, "This is the biggest load of shit I've heard all day. No one suspects me. I'm just not buying it."

He said, "Okay, Mallory. Maybe we can't arrest you. But we can tell you not to leave the city. And we can bring you downtown for questioning whenever the hell we want and have Gertie strip you naked and search every inch of your body with those cold rubber gloves. Maybe we'll take you down during Gertie's lunch hour. Maybe Dick and me will have to search your bod ourselves." I yawned and picked at my fingernails. Bucky just doesn't have it in him to play the bad cop. When he talks, his teeth stick out farther than his nose. Looking up at him from my chair, I could see all his fillings. I squashed out my cigarette.

Alex said, "Excuse me, but don't you feel embarrassed talking like that to a lady?"

Bucky said, "When I see a lady, then I won't talk like this."

I said, "Can we please get down to business? You want my file on Johann. Am I right?" Bucky flapped his teeth. I took this for an affirmative.

I said, "I won't give you that file."

He said, "If you don't give us that file, we'll get a court order."

"Then get it. And you won't see jack until then." By the time they got one, I could easily doctor the file. If I wanted to have anything to do with finding Belle's killer, I didn't want the cops in my way.

Dick came back. He saw the look on Bucky's face and said, "What, did I miss something?"

Bucky said, "She thinks we're walking out without that file."

Dick twisted his mustache and said, "Is that right, cupcake?"

I said, "There's nothing in it anyway. Just address and description. Nothing you don't have."

"We'll see about that." Dick walked behind my desk, pushed Alex out of the way, and opened my bottom drawer.

Alex said, "Don't you have to get a warrant, or is this just bad manners?"

Dick didn't look up. He rummaged around in my tampon box. He ordered Bucky to check the file cabinet. Bucky walked over and started to throw files on the carpet. Alex gasped and flung himself in front of the cabinet.

"You don't have to make a mess," he said. Bucky

pushed him away. Alex said, "Wanda, get over here and help me." I didn't move. I had a good reason.

Meanwhile, Dick was practically sitting on top of me, searching every drawer in my desk. When he came up empty he grabbed me by the shoulders, pinning me in my chair. He said, "Last chance, cupcake. Where is that file?"

"It wasn't in my desk? Then I haven't the faintest idea." I was more angry than nervous, but either way, I didn't want them to get any sense of me.

He shook me. Alex and Bucky stopped their pushing match by the cabinet to watch. Dick said, "Listen good, sweetie. I'm running out of patience here." His mustache twitched. "I don't give a flying fuck about your rinky-dink operation, and I don't give a shit about you. There's little stopping me from forcing you to turn over that file. And I think you know what I mean by forcing you."

I said, "If you lay one finger on me, he'll beat the crap out of you." I pointed at Alex.

Alex said, "Just give me five minutes to change into my black belt."

Bucky said, "Cool out, Dick. There's nothing here. Let's go talk to the judge." Dick didn't let go of my shoulders. I knew I'd get fingerprint bruises. He looked down at my face. I smiled.

"We'll be back in a few hours," Dick said threateningly. He released me and exchanged whispers with Bucky. Dick said, "We're going to be watching you, Mallory. Don't leave town." The office door slammed. I felt even more shaken than before, but at least there was some satisfaction in knowing they hadn't found the file. I'd been sitting on it the whole time.

Alex said, *"I'll* beat the crap out of *him?* No problem. He's only got a hundred pounds on me."

I stretched my shoulders. I found my Vans in my drawer and put them on without socks. I said, "I don't want to be here when they get back."

Alex said, "They won't be back today."

"Let's go anyway."

"You want to be alone?"

"Sort of. Don't take it personally."

"I never do," he said. I stood up. "No, I'll go," he said, and he left.

I lit a cigarette, letting the smoke roll between my fingers. Belle was dead. I could hardly believe it. I almost cried but stopped myself. I looked out my window and saw a gang of kids run out of a Korean deli. The manager chased after them. I wondered what they got away with.

CHAPTER TWO

THE REST OF A BAD DAY

The phone rang. It was Santina Epstein, the fiftyish, half-Jewish, half-Italian Fifth Avenue beautician who lives upstairs from me in Park Slope. The first dose of her yammering is the hardest to handle. I held the phone away from my ear.

". . . and your machine wasn't even on. I almost called the police, but Shlomo talked me out of it." Shlomo Zambini is Santina's doctor common-law husband. Santina continued, "You know him, Mr. Smartypants. He said to me, 'Leave her alone. She's a grown-up. If she doesn't have her machine on, it's probably because she doesn't want to talk to you.' Can you believe him? If it wasn't for those slim little hips of his. So perfect for . . . well, you don't want to hear about that. So anyway, this is the plan. Shlomo can't make it, so I'll come and pick you up at your office. I'd appreciate it if you can wait on the street for me. You know how I hate to park the car anywhere within twenty blocks of Times Square. All the garbage and bums and filth. The car is one thing, but my own safety, that's another story. The car's only money. All right, a lot of money. Just thinking about the Mercedes in Times Square gives me hives. And don't think I feel entirely comfortable with you waiting on the street either. But you insist you can handle yourself. God only knows why. It sends goose bumps up the back of my . . . I don't know . . . neck. Wanda, say something. It is you, isn't it? Alex? Is that you? Who the hell is this? I'm hanging up and calling the police right now . . ."

I said, "No, Santi. Please, whatever you do, do not call the police."

She said, "It is you. Why didn't you say anything, for God's sake? I almost had a coronary. Not as if I don't every day. You and that job of yours. Working in that horrifying neighborhood. One day something's going to happen—I just know it. If you'd only take a little money . . . or we'll send you to law school." Santina and Shlomo have a daughter fixation with me. Sometimes it's nice. Usually it's a pain in the gluteus. My real parents live in Miami; we don't talk much.

I said, "Santi. I'm okay. Everything is under control."

She said, "Okay, all right. Now, let's arrange a meeting time. You'll be on the corner of Broadway and 46th Street at, what's good for you? Let's say two o'clock? Sound good for you? That's good for me. And I don't want you taking any shortcuts through those broken-down buildings."

"You said that already. Look, Santi, I don't know

what you're talking about. Meet where for what reason? I'm busy today."

She said, "Oh, no, you don't, Ms. Professional Woman of the Year. You are having lunch with me today if it's the last thing you do. We made plans for this three weeks ago. This is my only day off all week. Check your book. Do it right now. I'll hold."

I pretended to check my book. There were files all over the floor. I said, "You're right, Santi. You're always right. But I really can't make it today. I have a headache. Another time—next week. Really."

She said, "Excuse me, Ms. I've Got More Important Things to Do, but who do you think you're talking to here? Okay, I understand. If you've got more important things to do, I'll have lunch at the salon with all those diseased, blue-haired women you know I love so much."

She sounded more upset than usual. "Santi," I said, "is there something you want to tell me?"

"What do you mean? I'm telling you my whole life story here, isn't that enough?"

I said, "Where's Shlomo? Is he coming to this lunch that's not going to happen?"

"No, actually," she replied, "and it doesn't have anything to do with you. You know Shlomo loves you very much."

"Santi, what?" I asked. It's not hard to tell when she's upset.

She said, "He's off at that greet-the-meat heaven, the Learning Annex, doing a sailing course. I spoke to him there. He just babbled about giblets or something. Wants to buy a yacht and dock it in Westport. I said to him, I said, 'You care more about this stupid course than you care about Wanda.' So he says to me, he says, 'Why is everything so extreme for you? If I knew that when I moved in,' yadda yadda yadda."

I said, "I think you mean jibs."

She said, "Giblets, jibs, whatever. All I know is that now I'm having lunch at the shop. I'll probably eat with Mrs. Berkenstein. You know her, blond, from the biggest bottle you could imagine. I've seen her pubic hair in the waxing room, and let me tell you, that woman is no blonde. I think she gets her hair done across the street. The only time I'd seen pubic hair that gray was on Shlomo's mother. That sounds pretty peculiar, doesn't it? Don't get any funny ideas. I saw her in the waxing room, too. So, a charming companion, that Mrs. Berkenstein. She's got three daughters on Wall Street. All making skillions of dollars a day. That'll be fine—lunch with Mrs. B. I'll love that."

Santina is an expert at emotional manipulation. I said, "What time do you want to come over?"

"What's good? One-thirty? I'll come up. See you then." She hung up. It was one o'clock. I could see her dashing out of the brownstone in her Indian summer mink. She'd drive to Manhattan like Guatemalan deer stampede to the scent of urine (something to do with psychedelic mushrooms; I learned about that in *National Geographic,* too). So Santi was coming to lunch. I scooped the files off the floor and dumped them into an empty drawer. She'd be here in twenty minutes; no more room to think about Belle. I killed the time flipping matchbooks into a hat.

She timed herself perfectly. She burst into my office, draped in mink, at exactly 1:30, per my desk clock. As always, she looked great. Perfectly coiffed and appareled. Feet made for two-tone slingbacks. Blond hair that looks natural. An incredible set of gams for a woman her age. Santi walks the loop around Prospect Park every day. She'd taken to wearing a velour sweatsuit lately. For someone with such a sense of fashion, you'd think she'd understand when I tried to explain that velour was out.

She sped toward me, momentum from the drive in from Brooklyn still firing her veins. She enveloped me in her arms.

She said, "You look like shit." Just having her arms around me spun me off on my first crying jag in years. Santi can get to me, even when she's being a pain in the thorax.

When I pulled away, after the tears stopped, Santina asked, "Baby, what's wrong?"

I couldn't speak from crying. She looked at me disapprovingly.

She said, "First, let's do something about this face. Then we can have a pleasant little chat." As she spoke she maneuvered me into my chair and sat down on my desk in front of me. She planted one leg on either side of me on the arms of the chair. Her pleated skirt dipped between her legs. She gently turned my head from side to side by the chin.

She said finally, "What have we here?"

I said, "Santi, please. Give me one small iota of dignity." Santina has makeover fits often. I never use the stuff.

She said, "Never." She inspected further. "Mmmm." She cocked her eyebrows. "You blotch from crying."

I said, "I like how it looks." She swooped the gigantic leather thing she calls a purse off the floor. She could reach it from the desk, that's how big it is. Inside it there was another bag that looked like a pair of summer squash squashed together. She held this squash thing in my face. She nodded knowingly.

She said, "Do you know what this is, Wanda?"

I said, "No. And I don't care."

"This is Santina's bag of tricks. The miracle maker. Otherwise known as a makeup kit. Now, let me take a better look at those eyes. You really should invest in some Niosôme eye creme. What a waste of a face. Ruining such natural beauty." She whipped out a wad of cotton and a mini-bottle of astringent. She said, "First of all, you must cleanse the skin. Makeup over dirt means blackhead before you can say pass the Stridex. But be delicate. Treat your face like a baby, caringly, lovingly."

She squeezed a generous portion (just like it says on the bottle) into the wad. Before she slathered I jumped up and walked across the room. There's only so much manipulation I will take. "I refuse to play a part in your Frankenstein movie. This is my face. Let's go have lunch. Now. I'm opening the door."

She fingered the wad. "Come here, Wanda," she said.

"No."

"Now."

I went back, and I sat down. I held my face up for her inspection. If she wanted to make a scene, fine. But she'd get more than she bargained for.

She wiped the wad on my face. It felt slippery and cold. It stung by my eyes. She doused the wad again.

"The last time I saw you cry was when you dropped my iron on your foot," she commented.

I liked the tingle on my skin. I said, "One of my clients was strangled to death last night."

Her hands dropped from my face. There was a moment of silence. Then she screamed, "That's it. That is it. No more. Do you hear me? No more of this bullshit detecting crap. I hate it. I will not, I refuse, I disallow you to continue this ridiculous waste of your brilliant mind. Absolutely not. Do you hear me? This will not go on for one more second. First we are going to move your stuff out of this pathetic office and away from this disgusting neighborhood. Shlomo will pay off your lease. Then you are coming to Brooklyn with me, and you and I are going to apply to every law school in this country until you get accepted to one. I'm going to lock you in your apartment and not let you out until you've finished your application essays. And then, in September, when we drive you to your new school, with all the car doors locked, I'm going to live in your dorm room and make sure you do all your homework. Then I'm going to sit on you until you get a respectable job."

I said, "Santi, calm down." She was taking the mothering too far.

"What happens if this strangler comes after you?" she asked.

I stood and said, "No one's coming after me. I'm not exactly the big time here." I swept my hand around the office. That quieted her for a second. "And I'm out of it anyway. It's not like Belle can hire me from the grave."

Santi said, "Thank God for that."

She tilted my head to the left and right, again by the chin. She put the stinger away and took out some coverup. "So, how's Alex?" she asked.

"Annoying."

"Lovers' quarrel?"

"We're friends."

"Shlomo and I thought you and Alex were an item."

I said, "Why would you think that?"

She said, "You spend so much time together."

"We work together," I replied.

She fussed with the makeup. "You've got such white skin," she said. "Alabaster. You look like you've been in prison. That's good, though. No wrinkles later. Stay out of the sun. Listen to me. This is my job. Believe you me, it's more fun to work on you for free than bleach Park Avenue la-di-da ladies at the shop. You don't need this goop on your whole face, just a few dots under each eye. Now, sweep the dots together. Gorgeous. Take a look." She held the mirror out in front of me. Under one eye there were three dots of nearly white coverup. She blended and showed me again. The eye looked cry-free.

I said, "Masterfully done, Santi." She went on, finishing my eyes and my mouth.

She said, "Alex. Alex. Now, let me see. A beautiful boy and a beautiful girl. You should be together. What wimps we mortals be. Me and Shlomo were friends first. For years. Of course I had to be the one to make the first move. Men are such cowards. Three weeks later he moved in. And believe you me, it wasn't exactly a move up for him."

Why do a rich beautician (they make more than you think) and a doctor live in a two-floor apartment in a pre-war brownstone in Park Slope? Why not the Upper East Side? The question Shlomo asks all the time. But Santina refuses to leave Brooklyn. She grew up there. She feels safer there. Or that's what Shlomo says.

I said, "I think Alex has a girlfriend."

"And?"

"I don't know her."

"Don't worry about other women. Eventually, you're only competing against yourself." Santi patted me on the head when she was finished. "All done."

"Thanks, Santi." I looked in the mirror in shock. I looked hot. I said, "You are a miracle maker."

"Enough simple pleasantries. How's biz?"

"You know, Santina, with Belle gone and all, I might have some trouble making rent next month. Do you think you and Shlomo—"

"Forget it. Over my dead body will you get one dime to save this hellhole."

"Don't hold back. Tell me what you really think," I said, smiling.

"You're not long for the detective world anyway," she commented. "You're too delicate."

I said gruffly, "I'm not delicate."

She fluffed her hair yet higher. "Can I have a ciggie?" When Santi feels especially daring she bums a cigarette from me. It's her way of rebelling. I gave her one. "You know, Wanda, even though you're out of danger for the moment, I still meant every word I said. I wish you'd stop with the crime fixation. Or at least go to law school and become a public defender. How can this satisfy you intellectually? I liked it better when you were a reporter. Thank God you're out of money. And don't come looking to Shlomo and me for any of that. I'm not giving you one red cent to revive this business." She puffed. "These ciggies make me feel giddy."

A giant light bulb went off in my head. Giddy. Skip Giddy. A former lover, and an editor at *Shinola* magazine. I'd met him at a publishing party for *Midnight*. Skip and Belle traded writers' names. I wrote a few crime stories for him myself when I was a reporter. And I spent a few nights with him. I hadn't spoken to him in six months. This could be it, I thought; I could get an assignment from him. I could do an obituary/crime piece on Belle. Beg for, what, 5000 words? Which means $5000. A kill fee for an advance—that'd be thirty percent—$1700. Enough to keep me going. And I *had* to save the agency, I thought guiltily, even if it meant doing it over Belle's dead body. I grabbed the phone and speed-dialed. Skip wasn't there, so I left a message. Santi was happily smoking on my desk. I went to her and kissed her on the cheek.

I said, "Another brilliant idea from you. How do you do it?"

She said, "What did I do?"

"You just saved Do It Right."

"I did?"

"You sure did."

"Shit," she said.

Skip called an hour later. Santi had one more flare-up before I sent her off. She promised not to upset Shlomo with her paranoia. Skip and I made plans to meet at Fanelli's in SoHo for a drink after work. I did no work; I played solitaire. At least I did reread all the transcripts and information I'd gotten on Johann and wondered if it was worth getting heat for. I thought about what I was going to say to Skip at dinner and what I'd wear if I were anywhere near my closet. I drank some Amaretto.

Skip and I had slept together three times on three consecutive nights one year ago. It was a torrid little affair that ended the usual way. I fell in love; he blew me off. For a while I called him during every major TV sporting event and made him talk to me for at least twenty minutes. Excellent revenge. When I got bored with that I stopped calling. He hadn't called me in all that time either. I still thought about him, though. I read his stories in *Shinola.* I had wet dreams about him. About the way he pressed my thigh with his palm. There was this gentle urgency to it. That's what I remember best about him.

Skip Giddy was Coney Island, Great Adventure, and the Bronx Zoo all at once. He knew his way around a woman's body like a butcher knows meat. I fell in a big way. I mean honeydew melons thrown off twenty-story buildings. I mean eggs on Halloween night. I mean a ton of bricks. I thought he had sparkling wit, a charming demeanor, a superior frontal cerebrum, and elegant taste. That all changed. In all fairness to Skip, he's not a bad guy. He just got scared. I would have, too, if I were he.

In the morning after our last night together, I woke him and said, "Skip—I want you to know that I really care about you."

He said, "I care about you, too."

"I want to marry you and have babies."

"Excuse me?"

"Lots of babies. Where should we send them to college?"

That was pretty much the end of things. After all this time I supposed I was over him. Yeah, like a barrel.

Indian summer clung like a wrap to the city. The night was warm. I decided to walk down to Fanelli's. New York during rush hour always turns me on. Hundreds of cars stuck in midtown traffic blare their horns. Prostitutes yawn in coffee shops, jerking their bodies awake with caffeine as they start their business day. The smell of dollar-a-bag honey-roasted pralines sweetens half the block. Boiled hot dogs stink up the other half. Homeless people begging for spare change and three-card-monte dealers seem to multiply in Times Square at 6:00. It's their bread-and-butter hour. Nine-to-fivers run for subway entrances, looking like hell and hating the world. The city stirs with the excitement of people desperate for some other life.

I fell into the rhythm of the street—no mind, all body—leaning left, leaning right, welcoming eye contact, daring anyone to brush my shoulder. Midtown fired my blood. The hysteria lessened as I headed downtown. People walked slower and said "excuse me" on the street. My blood slowed, too, and I started thinking again.

By the time I got to Fanelli's I was feeling the half bottle of Amaretto I had drunk at the office. It's sort of embarrassing buzzing on the sweet stuff. Skip was drinking a pint of Guinness when I walked in, sitting alone at a table. He didn't see me. It was crowded. The unusual usuals swarmed by the bar. I took a second to catch my breath—from the walk, and from the sight of Skip waiting for me. The lighting was sepia, like antique photographs. There was no music, only din. The night seemed warmer, or was that the body press by the bar? I waltzed up to him and said, "Warm or cold?"

He replied, "You know I drink it warm. You look gorgeous, Wanda. Have a seat." He smiled. He touched the small of my back when I sat down.

I said, "Thank you." I played it cool. I was after a job. But rational dealings with someone I want to screw usually prove difficult. He wore a black sports jacket, a *Shinola* T-shirt, and green army pants. He's about 5′9″, brown hair, stunning green eyes. Sort of balding, but in a cute preppy way. Which he is, preppy. He doesn't wear socks unless they're rag. He's got the preppy bone structure, but a little rounded, softer. His skin blotches in the wind. But it's his hands that melt my butter. They're long, tan always, and thin—the kind you fantasize on your breasts and all over your body. Those hands were on me. On the knee to get my attention. The hair under my jeans rose. I wished I'd shaved.

I ordered a margarita. He said, "Tell me about this story. It sounds perfect for *Shinola.*" *Shinola* is a hip, smart, ironic, and very funny New York magazine. But they do run crime stories, too. Just to spice it up.

I said, "I thought it'd be right for you."

He said, "No, wait. Tell me about that later. Tell me what you've been doing for the last six months." He acted nervous.

"The detecting thing. Not much else."

"Writing any?"

"No, but that doesn't mean I can't anymore."

"I didn't mean that. I thought . . . forget it."

"Thought what?"

He hesitated. My heart thumped. "This is hard to say. Seeing you makes it harder. I was going to call you today. I know you won't believe that, but I was."

I said, "I believe that. The cosmic spheres spin strangely."

He said, "Let me just say this before I chicken out. Oh, God, this is weird. I've been planning this for months, and now I've got to do it." He took a slug. "I've been working on some fiction these days. And you seem to come up a lot in my writing. I don't know if that matters to you, but with all the deconstructionalists I read in college, it means a lot to me. I wish I had a Wanda key on my computer so you could read what I've written and tell me what you think." What a shock. I loved it. Skip sipped his Guinness.

He said, "Okay. I've got to do my speech or I won't be able to get this out. See, I've been sleeping badly lately. Insomnia. And I stay up writing. I think about you in that way, and in another way. Two ways. The writing is the second way. The first way is kind of licentious. I hope you aren't offended by that." Hell, no. The more licentious, the better. I shook my head. Skip ran a finger along the top of his glass.

He said, "That's good. See, that weekend we spent together last fall meant a lot to me. I can't help feeling like it's fate that you called me today. I think that means something. Don't you? No, don't answer that yet. Jesus, I haven't let you say three words."

I said, "Keep going." I was skeptical, but it couldn't hurt to hear him out.

He said, "I know we haven't spoken in six months, but that's because I didn't think you wanted to hear from me. You were always so cold on the phone."

I replied, "That's because I wasn't ready to be hurt by you again."

He said, "You were hurt? I didn't know that. You always acted so coldly that I thought you hated me." Of course, I did hate him. But a male ego couldn't understand that. He continued, "I've had three pints already. I want you to know that. I would have said all this whether or not I had anything to drink. I want you to know that, too. But I am drunk enough to tell you that you look so beautiful that it hurts. I want to make love to you tonight. Think about how nice it'll be to wake up and have breakfast together."

I murmured, "Let's get out of here." A vision came to me: his hands, pressing into my thighs. If that was foreplay, I'm some slut.

He looked shocked. He said, "Do you really mean that? Where do you want to go?"

"Your place." He lives around the corner.

We left, giving the waitress a twenty. She smiled at Skip. How long had it been for me? Maybe four months? Five? I couldn't remember. The last lover I'd had was an ex-boyfriend from college days. He blew in, and out (as it were), for a weekend. It was unexpected, fun, and not worth recounting.

If Skip seemed too "peace, love, and flowers" that night, I excused him. He had just spilled major guts, for real or otherwise. I could always call him on it if he'd lied. And no one, not even the guy I'd wanted to see impaled with splintery spikes six months earlier, could lie about his writing and his fantasies. That would be some kind of sick blasphemy that he'd pay for in hell. But he couldn't be lying, I told myself. Even smoothies like him open up every once in a while.

We whizzed around the corner to his building. It was only dinnertime, and there were people on the street in T-shirts. Skip acted bashful as we walked to the third floor. He shares a loft. It's big, but not as big as my place in Park Slope. His floors are wood, and there's not much furniture. Very minimalist. All the curtains, covers, and walls are white. Books and magazines litter the floor, shelves, bed, bureau. The empty Chinese food containers on the kitchen counter were the only signs of untidiness, but even they blended in and looked artsy. I suppose the word for Skip's apartment is sterile. Or safe. I said, "Where's Burt?" Roommate.

He said, "Away for the week. Drink?"

I said, "You mean we're alone for the rest of the night?"

He said, "I don't need a drink either."

We converged on each other. And, like wild beasts in the jungle, we tore each other's clothes off. I'd always wanted to rip the shirt off his back, and I did. I tore that sucker in half. I chewed on his belt, I bit his stomach. I was happy.

He had me naked in seconds. We writhed around a bit, which was fun. I put his dick in my mouth. I sucked that thing like a golf ball through a straw. I could have sucked the liver out of him, but he detached himself. He held me up and looked me in the eye. It was an incredibly intense love look. Sort of sad, too. He kissed me on the lip and downward to my breasts. Finally they got the delicate attention they deserved. I felt Skip's hands. One was cupping my left breast, the other was creeping up my left leg: my wet dream. He massaged upward until his hand stopped right at my crease. He let it rest there. Just moving his fingers, kneading my leg muscle. We were kissing passionately, feeding off each other's mouths. He gasped, "Do you have any idea what you're like?" After an excruciatingly long time he placed his hand on me. I swooned. The lights were all on. I squinted at the ceiling. I looked down the length of my body, and I saw Skip's head between my legs. I felt clean and safe and let myself come. He pulled himself up over me and kissed me. He asked if I could taste myself, and I told him I could, and that it tasted good. Then we fucked.

One of my favorite baseball jokes is to say to a pitcher, "I like your motion on the mound." Well, Skip won his Cy Young Award that night. And at two in the morning, during our third inning, I understood what Belle meant when she said stealing home.

CHAPTER THREE

WHAT I'LL RESORT TO

I sleep on my back with my legs and arms stretched out. When I opened my eyes that Wednesday morning I saw a blurry, upside-down image of a man. I closed my eyes, one of which was sticky with sleep-glue, and rolled over. The bedcovers were bunched up at my feet. I opened my eyes again. The man was Skip. He was reading the *Mirror*. I touched my crotch and remembered the night before. I smiled to myself. To say Skip is good in bed would be the understatement of the century. We'd made it off the floor at some point the night before—I'm not sure when. It was somewhere between jungle beastdom and trench warfare.

My body felt damaged—bruises on the inner thighs, stiff legs and neck. The smell of coffee and sex assaulted my nostrils. My olfactory sense is sharp. Hard to believe for a smoker, I know. I spilled out of bed and slithered to the bathroom. I checked the mirror. The makeup had smeared, and my face looked almost patriotic with colorful touches of red lipstick, ivory smears, and blue popping veins. It must have been frightening for Skip to look at me. I left the bathroom and watched him reading and munching an apple. I sat on the futon. He didn't say anything at first. I didn't feel too good.

One of the best things about being self-employed is that I don't have to get to work by a designated time. I'm a night person. Alex usually opens the office and returns calls until I arrive. I wondered if he'd be there that morning. I felt a bit lonely. The clock by Skip's bed said 11:00 A.M. I asked, "Shouldn't you be at work by now?"

He said, "Personal day."

"What was your excuse?"

"I said that I was in bed with you and I had to fondle and squeeze and grope you for a while. And that I had to go to Belle's funeral. Get dressed. We've got three hours." He pointed at the announcement in the *Mirror*.

I felt a pang at the mention of Belle's name and the discussion of her corpse. I still couldn't believe it. I said, "Don't the police have to examine the body?"

"They're done. The paper says there were no alcohol or drugs in her bloodstream. Death by strangulation. Blah, blah, blah. You know all that already." He turned the page. "It says in the will that she wanted to do the Jewish thing. That means funeral the day after." Belle Beatrice from Greenwich was Jewish. She had converted; it's very New York.

I said, "The will?"

He quoted the paper, "To be read tomorrow morning at Barrister, Gladman & Blonder for involved parties." He put the paper down. "Think that means you?" Skip bit into the apple and looked at me. He said, "God, you look like hell."

I imagined Belle's assets. She was worth millions. To start, her parents are loaded. She had jewelry up the wazoo, and the million-five co-op on Central Park South. Southampton beach house. There was the magazine stock and its revenues. I speed-crawled to the phone by the bed, picked it up, and dialed.

Skip knew what I was doing. He sat next to me on the bed and leaned toward me. I cradled the receiver close to my ear so he couldn't hear. This at home in Brooklyn: "This is Wanda. Leave your name and take a number." Beep. Hang up. Hang up. "Wanda, this is Santina. Pick up the phone. I hope you and Alex talked. Maybe you're with him right now? Call with juicy details." That was it.

I called the office, but Alex didn't pick up. The message said: "You have reached Do It Right Detectives. Wayward spouse? Drug-abusing child? Need to know for your peace of mind? Please leave your name and phone number, and we'll get back to you. Thanks." Beep. "Hello, Ms. Mallory. Alan Gladman here of Barrister, Gladman & Blonder. I'm Belle Beatrice's lawyer. I found your number in Belle's address book. I expect you'll be at the funeral at Sleepy Homes today at two o'clock. Please allow time to be present at the will reading at our offices on West Fifty-Seventh Street tomorrow at nine A.M. sharp. I hope you are doing well, considering. Good-bye."

I said, "God, I may be golden."

"This funeral could be the social event of the season," Skip mused.

Suddenly I had to get out of there. "I have to go home and get dressed," I said. I hadn't thought about a will. Usually that's the first thing you think of when someone is killed. After sorrow, that is. I wondered if Belle would mind me thinking about her money, but I knew she'd do the same. If Belle had taught me anything, it was how to take care of number one. I was going to miss her.

"No, no. Let me take you to brunch," Skip said. "We can go to Agnès B. after. I'll buy you an outfit." Quite tempting, but I held my ground.

"Can't. I have to feed my cat." Otis hadn't had wet food since Tuesday morning. Or been cuddled.

"Let me come with."

"No, really. It's a private thing." I wanted to get away from him. The vibes weren't right all of a sudden. No one should be so good to me. Plus my apartment was messy as messy can be. Dirty underwear, cold pizza on the floor, overflowing ashtrays—very Oscar Madison. Otis and I like it that way. Whenever I do clean (which is usually for male company), Otis acts depressed for days. She pulls books off the shelf, and I have to spoon-feed her.

I got dressed, checked for Mama in my bag, and kissed Skip on the cheek. He grabbed me and kissed me more passionately. He mumbled something about not wanting to forget the fondling and squeezing portion of the afternoon. It felt good, certainly, but I didn't want him then. Maybe I'd had enough already. He told me he liked the soft part of my neck and happily proceeded to nuzzle. I wondered where the hard part of my neck was. Somehow in the cold light of morning his sincerity seemed less sincere. Feeling guilty about Otis and genuinely wanting to be alone, I moved away from him. Skip pulled me back. He kissed me again and twisted my curls.

I said, "I'm not into this."

He looked surprised. "I thought you liked it."

"I do."

"Then why not?" I wasn't thinking too clearly that morning. If I'd been more awake, and less distracted by the funeral, I could have explained myself to him. I thought of how little I trusted him, about how little I trust myself when it comes to sex. I was afraid I'd fall for him again. I remembered the way it had ended for us the year before, and how heartbroken I had been. But I didn't say anything. Skip took my lack of response as acquiescence. He kissed me and rubbed up against me. Not many women I know can walk away from a raging hard-on, even women with the purest intentions. But I'm no purist. And, that morning, I didn't walk away.

It was another beautiful Indian summer day. Brunch was nice. We strolled through Greenwich Village and had eggs Hussard at Aggie's on Houston Street. At my request we went to Betsey Johnson instead of Agnès B. I got a black cotton tit dress—not too sexy for a funeral, but enough to get a big smile out of Skip. We ran into Ecco for shoes. I got black suede pumps with a cutaway heel. Not exactly appropriate for such hot weather, but winter would be coming fast. The salesgirl told me that if I dyed my hair platinum, I could be the next Jayne Mansfield. Skip laughed when she said it and put his arm around my shoulder. We rode up to the funeral in a company car, courtesy of *Shinola.* I smiled a lot that morning. All very nice, but I couldn't get used to that kind of treatment. No self-respecting private dick does brunch.

The funeral home overflowed with mourners. People in black were crammed in the sedate outer chamber of the Sleepy Homes Funeral Parlor on 59th Street. There was a Central Park view from the front window, and I watched some of the horse-drawn carriages roll past. I stared at a man selling dime bags of pot at the corner of the park for a few minutes. I got bored and turned back to the people—chatting, cocktailing, giggling, gossiping. Skip was right; this could be the social event of the season. But the dignitaries, socialites, and publishing major-leaguers were all merely suspects from my point of view. Max Rudberg, president and CEO of the Foxboro Corporation—mega-global banking firm—twirled a Perrier by the door. Mr. Rudberg was about as attractive as the plague. Belle always complained that she could never lay him. I remembered saying, "What, with a bag on his head?" She laughed. Johann Pesto was there, too, looking innocent and sitting alone by the buffet table. I remembered that Belle had said he'd hurt her. I wondered how and to what degree. I'd keep my eye on him.

There was an old couple, shaken by sobs, accepting condolences near the entrance. Must be Belle's parents, I thought. Detective Dick O'Flanahey leaned against the bar biting olives. His partner, Bucky, had to be nearby, but I didn't see him. Dick spotted me. He smiled, winked, and twisted his mustache. Bastard. Bucky arrived next to him with a plate of hors d'oeuvres. I had expected the cops to show up. All these media giants were suspects to them, too.

Skip gripped my arm and steered me around. I was as anonymous as anonymous could be in that room. Skip, however, was not. People approached him constantly and said things like, "Skip, darling. Terrible about Belle. None of us is safe. By the way, have you read my rewrite?" or "Good to see you, Giddy. Didn't know you knew the deceased. I've known her for years, of course. I know everyone." Or, as one gorgeous young writer said, "Skip, hi. Where were you last night? I tried to call you ten times." He'd turned down his answering machine, but I'd heard it ring throughout the night. I thought, "So that's who it was."

Skip whispered as she slinked over to another young male editor, "Don't worry. She can't write her way out of a single-ply garbage bag."

I said, "That's some comfort. I'll just pretend she doesn't exhale lust."

The *Midnight* crew was there. The staff had changed a lot since I left, as is the way of magazine publishing, but I recognized the dedicated lifers sitting together in a corner. I wondered which one would inherit the magazine. There was Herb Stoltz, the managing editor. A child prodigy (Belle, being one herself, liked to surround herself with them) from Harvard. Tall, soft, and brown-eyed. Almost bearlike. He is perhaps one of the only straight single men in New York City who had turned Belle down, not once, not twice, but every day for three years. She treated him like a lost son with a latent Oedipal complex. He was twenty-nine to her thirty-five. She said to me once, back when I worked at *Midnight,* that she'd reached all her goals in life by the age of thirty-three with one exception. Apparently, she longed for the day when she could handcuff Herb to her bed and tease him mercilessly for two weeks. I asked her if she had a bedpan handy. I never desired Herb myself, if that says anything for my taste.

Next, Cheryl Stingon, the executive editor. The eruptive volcano under Belle's lava. At the magazine for all of its five-year existence. She's short, with matronly breasts, long black hair in a tight bun, and evil, twitching eyes. I always thought Cheryl was the queen to Belle's king, the one with the real power. While Belle went out to her endless lunches and lectures, Cheryl took over story meetings, approved covers and headlines. Belle wouldn't notice for a few weeks that Cheryl had gone over her head. Then she'd call her in for a chat. Things would be very Belle-oriented for a while afterward, but then the cycle would begin again. No one could figure out how Cheryl got away with it, or why Belle would allow it to happen. Usurping Belle's power was not something many people could get away with.

As for me, I didn't trust Cheryl. Nor did I like her. The key to office politics at *Midnight* was to keep on Cheryl's good side. She knew this better than anyone, and she waved her power around like a hammer. The day she decided she didn't like you, you could kiss yourself on the ass and wave good-bye over your shoulder. My number finally came up, like those of so many editorial serfs before me. She caught me on a minor fact-checking error. And when I say minor, I mean I published the wrong price on a dildo. That's why I left the magazine. She had it in for me, and I'm not one to postpone the inevitable.

Last was Ginger Jones, the staff writer. Physically a temptress. Tawny hair and skin, long and lean. And she always smells like lilies. She wrote most of the hard-newsy pieces *Midnight* ran: clitorial vs. vaginal orgasms; sex clubs in the city; the myth of ben wah balls. And she wrote erotica. Ginger's stories were always the hottest. At one point, right when I left, Belle told Ginger to settle down a bit and suggested she do some editing for a while. Belle was a writer herself, so maybe she was jealous of Ginger; or maybe she just wanted more writers' voices. Anyway, Ginger almost quit. Belle smartened up and gave her a raise. Also, the exclusivity clause was stricken from her contract; Cheryl's idea. Get her writing for other magazines and she'll cool out on *Midnight.* The plan didn't work, and Ginger's name became almost as synonymous with *Midnight* as Belle's. I always liked Ginger. She's a smart muffin. And, as I said, her stories were the hottest.

Skip cupped my ass to get my attention. "Ginger's looking pretty good, don't you think?" he asked. Suddenly I didn't like her so much.

Cheryl, Herb, and Ginger had their heads together, conferring. Some of the junior staff members fluttered near them, but the triad didn't seem to notice. I decided to approach them. I walked over and said,

"Hello. Good to see you all. I wish the circumstances were more agreeable."

Cheryl, all venom, spat out, "So, the prodigal princess returns." She gave me the once-over twice. She continued, "You're a day late." She didn't know about my detecting work for Belle.

Herb said, "Babe. You look dynamite. How's the crime business?"

I said, "As criminal as publishing." Herb laughed.

"Must we small talk?" Cheryl complained.

Ginger said cattily, "Wanda. I didn't expect to see you here. You haven't seen Belle in over a year, have you?" She didn't know either.

Herb said, "For Christ's sake. Both of you shut up. Wanda and Belle used to be close." Nor he. Belle may have kept a few secrets after all.

I said, "As a matter of fact, I was invited to come by Belle's lawyer. I hope I'll see you all at the will reading." Cheryl dropped her jaw. I turned and scouted for Skip. He was chatting up that gorgeous writer. He had his arm around her shoulder. She flipped her hair. He pushed it off her face. I made for the bar.

I ordered a margarita and sat down, alone against the wall. Dick and Bucky had disappeared, which was fine with me. I tried to use the time to examine the crowd for likely suspects, but there were too many distractions. Through legs and hips at eye level I saw Cheryl fuming in her corner. The writer with Skip pandered to him, and he ate it up. I noticed his eyes scanning the room. Probably for me. I sank into the wall; he didn't see me. I watched him lean close to the writer. He kissed her on the lips. Not an innocent kiss (not that innocent kisses exist for him), but a lingering meeting of lip-flesh. At a funeral. Had he no shame?

I eased up from my seat, feeling every moment of the previous night's passion in my sore thighs. I cursed myself for giving in that morning. I headed for the door. In my rush I bumped into the back of a big man in a black suit. He was at least six-five, with long blond hair. It was Johann Pesto.

He took a good look at my tits and said, "I don't believe we've met."

I said, "Wanda Mallory—distant relative of the deceased. And you are?"

"Johann Pesto. Grieving fiancé." He didn't seem too upset.

"This must be difficult for you."

He replied, "I'm dealing as best I can. But the loneliness is so painful."

"You'll be fine. Time heals."

"You could help heal me."

Out of the corner of my eye I caught Dick and Bucky watching by the buffet. I said, "I'll take a rain check. Excuse me." The last thing I needed was further association with Johann Pesto. At least for the moment.

I made for the door, but Skip stopped me. He put his arm around my waist and said, "Where're you going, angel food? The event just started."

"This isn't an event, it's a funeral," I retorted.

"What's wrong?"

"Would it be possible for you to keep your hands off other women when you go out with me?" I asked.

"Of course, love cake. I didn't know you cared."

I said, "Well, I don't." He leaned over and kissed me. I felt a tug from my belly button to my clit.

He whispered, "I think you care."

A tall man in a black double-breasted suit announced that the funeral was about to begin. All the publishing gods and society doyennes crammed into the antechamber, and into the pews. The room was nice; it felt like a theater. Belle's closed casket sat on a table in the front—the stage area. I sat in back so I could get the best view. Johann sat in front. As he walked by me he let his hand brush over my shoulder. Skip didn't notice. The *Midnight* crowd sat in the first row, next to Belle's parents. Dick and Bucky stood by the doors in back. I put on my glasses.

The funeral director began solemnly. He told us all of his personal grief for all the setting suns who'd passed through his doors. He pointed at Belle's casket and read a short bio. Then he turned the podium over to Herb Stoltz. I should have guessed he'd speak. I'd noticed his stack of index cards earlier when I spoke to him. Herb nodded to the crowd and began.

"We all want this to be short. I personally have never understood this ritual for the dead. It seems to cause more pain than solace. We all loved Belle. That's why we're here, putting ourselves through this. We eat the crudités, we drink the wine, yet we taste nothing but the bitter passing of a friend. I promised myself that I wouldn't bring up the baffling circumstances surrounding Belle's death, but only the astonishing accomplishments of her life. But I never thought I'd be here this Wednesday, October seventeenth, at her funeral. I've prepared a eulogy, and I guess I'll just read it to you now." Herb shuffled his cards. He took a sip of water.

He continued, "How to measure the erotic tug of one single corn-silken hair? I bask in its glow as I look down at the top of her head. Her lips caress my throbbing ache as tiny bits of corn silk stick to my—" He stopped suddenly. He blushed and looked up. There was murmuring in the antechamber. Skip leaned over me.

"Why didn't you tell me Herb and Belle were doing it?" he said, and he gently licked my ear. He said, "That last part turned me on. What do you think the corn silk was sticking to?"

The whole room was abuzz. Herb started protesting, "I don't know what this is. It got slipped into my speech. I did not write these words." Dick and Bucky rushed the dais and snatched the card from Herb's hand. Dick held on to Herb's lapels while Bucky told the mourners to settle down. There was some hushed talk by the dais until Herb and the cops split a few minutes later. I wanted to go after them, but Skip held me back. "You won't learn anything from them right now," he cautioned me, "but there's still lots to be seen here." He was right. I guess that was why I decided to put up with Skip for a while longer—for his moments of perception. And the sex, of course.

The remainder of the funeral proceeded without incident. A rabbi spoke, the one who had converted Belle. And Belle's mother managed to get out a few words. Johann looked back at me once or twice, but not as often as Cheryl looked at Johann. The service lasted about an hour. I was one of the first to leave. I told Skip that I had to go to the office immediately, and he didn't seem to mind. I noticed Cheryl and Johann flirting on my way out.

I was staked out on West 59th Street behind a streetlight, waiting for Johann. I saw Skip get into a cab with the lust-oozing writer. I smoked a cigarette down to the filter. When I saw my mark I made my move.

Johann hopped a taxi solo. I waited until it pulled out. Then I jumped into the next available one and instructed my driver to "follow that cab." (At times like this I reminded myself of Columbo.) I didn't know what Johann had in mind when he asked me to heal him, but I was determined to find out. I figured I owed Belle enough to uncover what the Swede was really after.

I followed Johann to Times Square, where he got out of his cab. It was bustling as usual during rush hour. I watched as several women and homeless people approached Johann. He waved them off. If anyone bothered me, I didn't notice. Johann crossed the street and stopped in front of a strip joint called the Orchid Lounge. He checked a matchbook from his pocket. Then he ducked in.

The Orchid Lounge is a bottomless bar. People are always handing out fliers about it on the street. It's as sleazy as clubs get in Times Square. The waitresses wear tops, but they don't wear bottoms. Thus the name of the joint. I walked over to the entrance. The two bouncers were pro-wrestling types. They stood like totem poles on either side of the door. One wore a sleeveless T-shirt that said "Manny's Gym. No place to hide. Nowhere to run. Not for everybody." They tried to keep me out, assuming I was free-lance. I slipped them a twenty each and slid in. I was still wearing my tit dress from Betsey Johnson. Not too far from appropriate attire. And isn't that the wonder of today's fashions—one moment funeral garb, the next, slutwear.

The lights were dim, the music pulsing and loud. The wood tables had cigarette scars. Colored jalapeño-shaped bulbs hung on the ceiling, like Christmas in Mexico. S & M porn videos were projected on the walls. If anything rattled me about the joint, it was the videos.

I saw Johann sitting at the far side of the circular bar. He ordered a Dewars, rocks, no fruit. He checked his watch and arranged his tie. He glanced sideways at the babes taking orders. I sat on the other side of the circular bar and watched him simmer for a few drinks. When I'm on assignment I drink vodka. When I'm not I drink tequila. That night I was drinking bloodies. Johann seemed to be waiting for someone. So I was too. The toothless owner/bartender/pimp came over and introduced himself as Luigi. He asked if I'd ever been in before. I told him no. He said he was sure he knew me; after all, tits like mine were hard to forget. I thanked him and kept my eyes on Johann.

Luigi was telling me a story about two sisters from Nantucket when the woman came in. All the men around me turned to look. Even Luigi paused. She approached Johann. She was tall and zaftig in a beautiful red dress. Modest heels. I'd guess thirty-two or -three, long brown hair and olive skin. Someone near me muttered the word yummy.

I was wearing my glasses so I could see perfectly.

Johann smiled when he saw her. He motioned for the lady in red to sit. She pulled back the bar stool next to his, but he grabbed her by the elbow and turned her around to sit on his lap. He put his arms around her waist. I could hear her giggle and squeal from across the bar. She turned toward Johann and rubbed his cheek with hers. They looked like two big cats preening. I felt like a voyeur, but all good detectives should have some of that in them. He bounced her on his knee. They talked. I couldn't see their mouths too well. Luigi's face was in the way. I could see *his* black hole of a mouth just fine. I smiled and nodded and let him pour the bloodies.

Johann and the woman were deep in conversation. He began to look concerned. I kept myself from making any conjectures; I focused on specific action. She shook her head at something he said. He looked sad. She petted him on the head like a dog. He smiled weakly. She spoke, and he nodded unconvincingly. She gestured gently, accenting words with her hands. He grabbed her wrists and she play-struggled a bit. Then the kiss. A nice kiss. Not the kind you'd expect in a place like the Orchid Lounge. I started to imagine what they might mean to each other, and if she was into vibrating eggs, but I stopped myself. The kiss ended. I picked up my drink and got up, interrupting Luigi's story about his mother and a sailor. I told him I was off to the little general's room. He laughed.

The long walk around the bar was fraught with obstacles. I dodged drunks, random hands, and grabs. I felt a bit slimy. I tucked my glasses into my bag; I'd be able to see close up. Johann and the woman were still talking when I made it over. I sat down on the stool she'd almost taken. She climbed off Johann's lap and stood between us.

I said, "Excuse me, is this seat taken?" Her eyes were hard, but her face and mouth were delicate.

She spoke with perfect enunciation. "It appears so," she said, "by you." She smiled—perfect teeth.

Johann said, "The girl from the funeral. What a nice surprise."

I sipped my bloody. "Come here often?" I asked.

The woman said, "You two know each other? How perfect for us."

I said, "We just met today."

Johann said to the woman, "At the funeral."

She got nervous suddenly. "Who are you?"

"Just a distant relative," I replied. "I hardly knew Belle."

She smiled and nodded at Johann. She asked him excitedly, "Did you set this up for me? You big Swede."

He said, "I just had a conversation with this lady. Did you follow me here?" He didn't seem pleased.

I said, "Just a happy coincidence. Cosmic spheres spinning."

"I know you did this for me." She turned to me and said, "Isn't he the sweetest?"

I said, "I'll let you know once I've tasted him." She loved that; she nearly squirmed out of her clothes.

Johann said, "Martha. I'm not sure this is such a good idea."

"Hush now. I'm having a conversation with this young lady."

I was frantically trying to devise a plan. I still didn't

know what they had in mind, or what she meant by saying he set this up. It occurred to me that they might be killers.

Martha looked me up and down. "Now, tell me, what brings you here—or, more specifically, what brings you to this stool?" She gestured with a sweep at all the empty stools around the bar.

"You look like a nice couple," I replied.

"Swing?" Martha asked.

What an antiquated word, I thought. Playing along, I said, "Whenever I can."

Johann fidgeted in his seat. This was not the direction I'd hoped this conversation would take. Johann, my mark, was barely speaking. I figured I'd lose them once we got outside.

She said, "How about right now?" Martha spoke up. "Right here." Green light: escape to the bathroom imminent. Johann looked terrified. His eyes implored Martha. I decided to get out before things got strange. I made a last-ditch attempt.

"Why don't we run out and get some props?" I said brightly.

Martha said, "No. Right now."

Johann grimaced. "Martha, this is silly," he muttered. Martha waved his comment off. He whispered to her, "I love you." I almost felt sorry for him. She mumbled an encouragement. "Okay. I'll do it," Johann acquiesced. "But don't make it hurt."

I decided it was time to go. I jumped up, but Martha grabbed my hand and placed it on Johann's crotch. Nothing there; or, rather, no interest was evident. I pulled back. She put her own hand over mine and pressed into Johann. She was stronger than she looked. She kissed him, like before, on the lips. Against his will he responded. She leaned into him and kissed him more passionately. I watched as if it wasn't my hand on his dick. I could feel him get more and more hard. She seemed to be getting pretty hot herself. Despite myself, I was fascinated. I couldn't figure this out. She needed someone else to be turned on? Her idea of an experiment? Who was she, anyway? Her clothes said money, and her face was proper. Yet here she was with Johann in the Orchid Lounge. Could they only meet in places like this for fear of being recognized? Martha moved my hand away. She held on to my middle finger as she yanked Johann's fly open. Johann looked pained. The face of someone having his thumbs screwed or someone in desperate need of an orgasm.

When Martha managed to unzip Johann completely his cock jumped out as if jerked by a string. Never loosing her grip on me, Martha placed my hand on him and covered my hand with hers. Our hands pulled on him. I looked at Luigi across the bar. He saw what was going on and held his drink up to salute me. I felt slimy. Other people were watching, too, and rubbing themselves under the table. I felt even slimier. Bottomless waitresses whizzed by, their trays loaded down with boilermakers, too jaded to rubberneck. Suddenly Martha fell to her knees and started sucking on him. Johann groaned and put his hands on her head. I began backing away from the bar. We made eye contact; again he had that pain/pleasure look. When he came he closed his eyes and opened his mouth, his blond hair cascading back like silk. Someone at the bar applauded. Martha rose and looked for me. By then I was at the door. As soon as I got outside I hailed a cab and sped home to Brooklyn. I'd had enough for one evening. I wondered if Alex was having as much fun.

I didn't get much sleep that night. I called Alex half a dozen times, but he never picked up. Must have been at the girlfriend's. Skip called and asked if he could accompany me to the will reading. I told him Alex was going with me. When I couldn't reach him by eight the next morning I got dressed to face the symphony alone. I went classic—Ann Taylor blue and black skirt, black blouse, and my new Ecco shoes. I even shaved my legs.

Barrister, Gladman & Blonder had a whole building on West 57th Street. Gladman's office was on the seventh floor. A nice old lady named Emily buzzed me through glass doors. I was ten minutes early. Lawyers in three-piece suits sped around in the corridor, secretaries chasing after them jotting down their every utterance in steno pads. Paralegals were lined up at the Xerox machines in the hallway. I rounded the corner toward Gladman's office. Someone beat me there: Johann was pacing outside, fuming and smoking Dunhills. I spotted him before he saw me, so I had time to hide in an empty conference room. I decided to wait for the others to arrive.

At two past nine I entered the room. They were all there: Cheryl, Ginger, Herb, Dick and Bucky, Mom and Dad, and Johann. Herb seemed to have recovered from the eulogy incident, but he had one eye on the cops. Cheryl was sitting next to Johann, thrusting her old-maid tits at him. He responded politely. When he saw me his face turned gray. I took a seat in back, glasses on. I assumed that the man with Coke-bottle glasses behind the big oak desk was Alan Gladman. I vaguely remembered seeing him at the funeral. He was dressed lawyerly in a tweed three-piece. His hair was black and slicked back. I guessed he was late forties. The office was replete with framed hunting paintings, green Tiffany lamps, and an antique grandfather clock leaning against wood-paneled walls. His desk blotter was even bigger than mine. I didn't think it possible. Even with all those chairs, the office was spacious and somber. It had the right feel for a will reading.

Gladman said, "Everyone present?" He counted heads. "Do we all know one another?"

Johann said, "Just read the damn will."

I turned to him. He avoided my eyes. I looked over at Belle's parents. They were clinging to each other. It was graveyard silent in the room before Gladman said, "Very well. Formalities aside, this is the last will and testament of Belle Beatrice. Written just last week, I might add. You can't say Belle didn't know a thing or two about timing. No, you can't say that."

Ginger shifted in her chair ahead of me, and I caught the scent of lilies. "Please, Mr. Gladman," she said, "we're all a bit anxious."

Gladman said, "Yes, yes. Forgive me. Just trying to make this as pleasant an experience as possible. These are troubled times. Women can never be too safe in modern society. Belle may have learned her last lesson too late. Well, you all know why we're here." Gladman inspected his glasses. He cleaned them. He replaced them. "Now. The will states as follows: 'This is my last will and testament. I don't want to get into all the sound mind and body business. You all know my intellectual and physical states of being. And that they are exceptional. Not to boast from the grave or anything. I'm not all that sure that I'll be dead before I rewrite this will. But don't any of you try to contest this. If I'm dead when this is read to you, this is what I want at this time. So no funny stuff. First of all, about the funeral. Make it the day after, please, as is the tradition of my faith. Not too grand an affair. Something nice and small. Maybe a few hundred of my closest friends and admirers. I would like to be cremated, if that's all right with my parents. Have my ashes placed in an urn and give it to them. Hi, Mom and Dad. I hope you're doing okay. I decided to leave you all of my personal possessions—my co-op (you always wanted a pied-à-terre you could be proud of) and everything in it. You will also get the house in Southampton, and everything in that. I'm not leaving you any money. I think you have enough. It's sort of peculiar for the brood to leave money to the parents anyway. A bizarre flip-flop on things. To my lover and friend, Johann Pesto, the man I've come to care deeply for in such a short time, I leave you my love, some superb memories, and $500. I know it doesn't seem like much, and it certainly isn't, but I don't feel comfortable leaving you more. I'm sorry. I've only known you for a few weeks. You are extraordinary in the sack. Take the $500 and buy a suit. You could have a future as a gigolo. I hope you understand.'" Cheryl wriggled in her seat. She was obviously getting some ideas.

Gladman read on: "'About the magazine. I don't

want any outsiders to come in. You get that, Herb? No one is to buy the magazine and make it some lewd travesty. Some piece of pornographic crud. Just picture me spinning in my grave. All of my stock in the magazine (which is fifty-one percent) is to be placed into a trust. Gladman, you see to it that no one gets his hands on the principal. The dividends are to be used once a year on a massive party celebrating the magazine and in memory of me. Cheryl, do with the magazine what you will. It's your baby now. And I trust you will be faithful to my vision. Give yourself a big raise. And give Ginger a raise, too. Herb, you are to become president of the company. As it exists now, Beatrice Publishing Inc. is just *Midnight* magazine. The remaining forty-nine percent of the stock is held by the company. Take that money and expand. Create a magazine group, or publish a book. Whatever. In effect, you will be Cheryl's boss. And she will answer only to you. Pay yourself what you see fit. The company is in your able hands, and I trust you will continue the success of the magazine for many years.' "

Gladman paused for a sip of water out of the tumbler on his desk. Cheryl got up and slammed the door behind her. Gladman watched as she left the room. He said, "She sprang out of that chair like a bamboo shoot. I presume that was Cheryl Stingon?"

Herb said, "That's right."

Gladman shrugged. "Well, on with the will. 'The remainder of my money, including all stocks (besides the magazine stocks), which are to be liquidated immediately, will go to pay off my debts on the co-op and house, jewelry, minks, and cars so my parents don't have to worry about silly bills and mortgages. I also want you to set up a fund for a yearly fellowship of $7,500 to be given to a graduating female journalist student at Dartmouth of considerable merit who has a healthy sex life. Call it the Belle Grant. Let the female professors of the English department choose the student each year. They'll like that. That should leave about $500,000. Here comes the tricky part: For the past few weeks, a sense of dread has enveloped me. I know it sounds odd, but I have this feeling something bad may happen. That's why I wrote this will. If I should, by any chance, die unnaturally, all that money should go to my friend and protégé, Wanda Mallory, if she is able to uncover the circumstances of my death. If I'm dead when you hear this (and why else *would* you be hearing this?), something fishy will have happened. If so, Wanda will receive this money once the circumstances are uncovered. I repeat, Wanda will receive *no* money until the crime is solved. And because Wanda has always had such trouble with deadlines and diligence, I want to make this interesting for her. If she is unable to solve the crime in one week's time, the $500,000 will be divided up between the New York Public Library (and Gladman, get them to put *Midnight* on microfiche) and the New York Historical Society. Sorry, Wanda. But that lazy streak in you has just got to go. And I can think of no better way to see you jump than solving my murder, if indeed that happens. Thanks, everyone. I hope you are dealing well with my death and are pleased with the contents of this will. Of course, if nothing happens to me, your satisfaction won't be an issue. And if you're not pleased, then you deserve what you got.' "

I could almost see her chuckling when she wrote that. Belle's trademark last laugh. My mind spun—$500,000 would save the agency, and I'd get my revenge on Belle's killer. I had to get going, to think up some ideas fast.

Gladman put the document back in its folder. He rested his eyes on each of us for a few seconds. Then he said, "Belle has made me executor of her will. It won't take too long to sort out all the legal rigamarole. I'll be contacting you all in the upcoming week to discuss the details. Any questions?" He scanned the room. "Fine," he said. He buzzed his intercom and told his secretary to bring in some coffee. Coffee. I knew well enough to stay away from that for a while. I had a crazed week ahead of me.

Mom and Dad were shuddering. Herb wore a secretive smile. Johann looked as though he wished there were a rock handy to crawl under. A hidden door to the office slid open behind me. I heard the secretary walk in. I was watching Johann at the time. He seemed to twitch.

A distinctly familiar voice said, "Shall I put this here, Mr. Gladman?" My memory clicked, and I wasn't surprised at all when I turned to look.

Mr. Gladman said, "Yes, Martha. Right here is fine."

CHAPTER FOUR

THE BIRTH OF AN INVESTIGATION

The sun belly-flopped into the Hudson. I had downed two eggs at a coffee shop near the office after the will reading. I spent the rest of the afternoon trying to get in touch with Alex and making a list of possible suspects. I also spent some time flipping matchbooks into a hat. I was getting pretty good at it.

Around 7:00 I headed home to change into less conspicuous garb for the night's sleuthing. I planned to go after Johann. I took my usual shortcut between two construction sites on 43rd Street to the D train entrance. There were a few homeless people sleeping under newspapers when I got off on the 7th Avenue platform in Brooklyn. One asked me for spare change. I replied, "Who has spare change?" and gave her a quarter. I lit a cigarette and shuffled down Flatbush Avenue. There was a man shouting up a fire escape to another man on the second floor of a building on my block. He was saying, "You got a quarter?" For a minute I thought he was talking to me.

I said, "You're five minutes too late." He gave me a crazy look. The man on the second floor threw down a small glass vial. I realized the first guy didn't want change. As I got closer to my brownstone I saw the light on in my front window. I never leave my lights on. I sat on the stoop for a few minutes and finished my cigarette. It tasted swell. I went inside the building, Mama rooted solidly in my hand. I kicked my apartment door open. Spinning with detective finesse, I swept the living room with the .22. No one in sight. I heard water running. I inched gingerly toward the back of my apartment, gun forward, to the bathroom. Someone had been there all right. The place was fastidiously clean. Otis was nowhere. My heart thudded under my mammaries. Radiator pipes banged.

The floorboards creaked as I walked back. I heard Otis cry. If anyone messed with the cat, I'd be obliged to splatter gray matter. On the threshold of the bathroom now. The door was closed. A steady stream of water was running inside. Steam oozed out under the crack. I banged the door open with my shoulder and rotated, legs spread. Otis shrieked like a battered child and ran out between my legs. Through the mist I saw his outline. The fog flowed out the open door, and I got a better look. The man was kneeling by the tub. I had the gun pointed between his eyes. The power rush was delicious, but I didn't give in to it. He sprang at me. We wrestled for control of the gun. He had me pressed against the toilet. He bent my arm back, and my elbow hit the handle. The toilet flushed. His mouth was inches from mine. He smiled and took the gun away. He released me. I walked out of the bathroom.

I went in front to the kitchen and poured myself a stiffy. The sound of water stopped. Aiming a gun and not firing is like fucking all night and not coming. I pulled long and hard on my tequila and Rose's lime juice, smacking my lips. He came up behind me and said, "You scared the shit out of me."

I said, "Alex, what are you doing here?"

He shrugged. "Cleaning. What happened at the funeral with Herb? I saw the *Mirror.*"

I gave a look that said I didn't want to talk about it.

"I tried to call you." He flopped his hair to one side.

I said, "Did you have to twist my arm back there?"

"Any excuse to touch you," he commented sarcastically.

"I could have shot you, you know. What the hell were you doing anyway?"

"Just rinsing out the bathtub. You had soap scum."

I freshened my drink and faced him.

He said, "Santina let me in. We cleaned . . . with Clorox."

"So I smell." I took a slug.

"I've been alone in a darkroom all day. I wanted to find out what happened today. You seemed so upset when I left—I was worried." He gestured for a drink and said, "If you want me to go, I'll go."

I didn't reply. I poured a drink and handed it to him. I strolled into the walk-through living room and lay down on my belly on the couch. He'd even fluffed the pillows. "Five-second back rub?" I asked. Alex downed his drink and came over to me. He lifted the back of my Ann Taylor and proceeded to massage.

Alex is the ultimate five-second rubber. When I have my druthers, he lasts ten minutes. He mumbled questions about what happened, what the *Mirror* had reported. It was obvious the paper had blown Herb's slip-up out of proportion; I'd have to correct him. I only had a week to solve the case, but for the moment, Alex's knuckles cracking my spine were all I could focus on.

The phone rang, and I asked Alex to get it. He picked it up and said, with fifth-gear charm, "Hello?" I hoped it was Skip. It wouldn't hurt him to hear a man answer my phone. Alex said, "Yes, Santina. She's home, but I've already put her to bed. . . . Yes, she seems more relaxed. . . . No, she loves the cleaning we did. She said she'd come up and thank you tomorrow. . . . Okay, Santina. Good-bye." He hung up.

"She told me to tell you that law school applications are due in two months." Without giving me a chance to speak he resumed rubbing and kneading and tearing my back muscles into a shredded lump. It felt swell. He continued, "In case you haven't seen the paper, I've got a copy. And I fed the cat." I muttered Thanks and began drifting off into P.I. slumberland. I had a notion before I slept: It seemed that whenever I wanted to be alone someone popped up. It wasn't always a bad thing. I made a mental note to buy some makeup for my eyes. I thought I felt Alex brush my cheek with his lips before I lost consciousness, but it was probably wishful thinking.

The next thing I remember was waking up at 6:30 A.M. Otis dive-bombed from my dresser onto my stomach—her subtle way of expressing hunger. I kicked back the covers of my bed. Alex must have carried me to my bedroom Tarzan-style. That might do wonders for the normal girl's ego, but I didn't like it. I could do just fine on my own. I padded out to the kitchen. My back ached. Mornings and I have never gotten along. Otis dares to wake me at the first blink of dawn most days. I'm semi-used to it.

Alex, morning person, was asleep facedown on the couch in boxers. He does have a cute bod. Long, thin legs. I like long legs, and slim hips—all the better for the equestrian thing I'm so fond of. I imagined riding Alex but stopped myself quickly. My fantasies have a way of taking me over, and I reminded myself that he wasn't available for that. I fed the cat and started brewing some coffee. Yes, coffee. Shocking my system into attention wouldn't be a terrible thing. Alex roused on the couch, modestly grabbed his pants off the floor, and held them against his privates. I said, "What, you think I've never seen boxers before?"

He laughed and let his pants fall away. I saw it wasn't the boxers he was hiding. But don't all men wake up with chubbers? Or is that just when they sleep with me? I turned back to the Mr. Coffee so as not to embarrass my cohort. I said, "We've got a lot of ground to cover today. Let's do the Last Hours of Her Life research first. Belle left me at 3:00 P.M., and the police estimated the time of death to be before midnight. That's at most nine unaccounted-for hours."

Alex rubbed his eyes and said, "We're investigating the murder? What time is it?"

I said, "We're six and a half hours into the first day of the investigation." Or the second. I'd have to check on that. Adrenaline ricocheted through my veins. Mornings be damned; there was $500,000 at stake here. Otis purred ferociously after her main course—liver and kidney puree. It takes so little to please her.

Over coffee I filled Alex in about all the events since I'd last seen him, leaving out the sex-god Skip part as much as possible. Alex agreed to put his portfolio work on hold for the week to help with the investigation. I made toast.

We ate. After, I said, "Isn't it just like Belle to stick me with a deadline? One week. That's like pissing on a forest fire."

Alex said, "At least you're getting your sense of humor back. I bet it's because you're torn between your sadness and your resentment for Belle."

I said, "Are we going to explore my psyche, or find a killer?"

We figured out a plan. We were to go to *Midnight* first and lie in wait for Cheryl and Herb. We wanted to talk to them, since Belle probably went back to the office after my lunch with her. But how to handle the Swede? And how to get at Martha? (If she recognized me at BG&B, she didn't show it. Johann must have warned her.) We decided to wrap our minds around that later and stick like Skippy to the *Midnight* crew. The sun came in my front window. Someone rattled garbage cans on the street. It looked like another perfect day.

"I refuse to talk to you in any context, language, or about any subject." Cheryl Stingon had a broomstick up her butt as usual. She didn't have an office door to slam, so she suffered the quiet indignity of allowing our eyes to follow her as she strode back behind her desk and frumped into her swivel. Her office was bigger than the average cube. It was cluttered with magazines and memos and manuscripts. Cheryl was dudded to the hilt in black. She actually looked good—spinster tits and all. Alex was dressed per normal in 501s and a white T-shirt. I was wearing a cute flower skirt from Betsey Johnson with my lace T-shirt. I wore my Vans—I knew I'd be running around.

I said, "When are you moving into Belle's office? Need any help?"

She said, "Mind your own beeswax." I hadn't heard that one in a while. Alex poked me in the ribs and motioned down the hall. Herb was coming our way. Alex went over to start him up.

I went into Cheryl's cube and sat down across from her. Her hair was yanked tightly off her face like the Princesse de Clèves. Courtesans in the sixteenth century used to die from having their hair tied so tightly (I learned about that in my *Fun Factoid Almanac*). Cheryl was doing her best to ignore me, typing furiously on her IBM-compatible. It looked like she was writing a memo to the staff about the forthcoming changes at the magazine. I said, "Cheryl, why don't you like me?"

She stopped typing. Her look could have curdled sour cream. She spat out, "Everything just falls into your lap, doesn't it? I'm not going to do a damn thing to help you get that money." Cheryl must have been briefed about the close of the will reading. She resumed playing the PC keyboard.

I whipped out my steno book. "What happened when Belle returned from lunch on the day she was killed?" I demanded.

"God, can't you take a hint?"

I plopped my steno in my lap—thwap. I said, "You should like me, Cheryl. I'm literate. I'm a fashionable gal." Cheryl grimaced at me. I picked up a pile of the papers on her desk. Some were letters addressed to Belle. She stopped typing. I said, "What's this? Going through Belle's stuff?"

She barked, "I was instructed to clean out her desk."

"Instructed by whom?"

"Give me back those papers." She reached for the pile, and I leaned back.

I said, "Not so fast." I quickly flipped through. One of the first letters I saw caught my attention.

I read out loud: "Ode to Belle's Behind: The twin melons sway and bob, like wind through the garden of my heart. They bounce under a thin veiling of silk, and my breath goes aflutter. Her melon cheeks are ripe—I know because I squeezed them."

Cheryl said, "What is that?"

"Is it just me, or does that sound like the thing Herb read at the funeral? Which brings up an interesting issue: Didn't I see you going through Herb's index cards before the service?"

"No. And I have no idea what that is." She pointed at the poem in my hand.

"You didn't have a little crush on Belle, did you?"

She stood and pointed the way out. I took the cue. I said, "We'll talk later."

"Much," she said.

I went into Herb's office. Cheryl's a tough bird, like a Pathmark chicken. Belle got along wonderfully with her. Maybe better than I thought.

Alex was asking the basics when I went in. Herb the bear greeted me with a hug and apologized for the mess. He said, "I'm moving into Belle's office this afternoon." I sat on the arm of Alex's chair, across from Herb.

Alex said, "The body's not even cold yet."

"She was cremated," Herb replied.

"Where's Cheryl going to sit?" I asked.

Herb said, "She's going to stay in her office. I had her clean out Belle's desk this morning." That explained her pleasant mood. Herb continued, "I've just been telling Alex about when Belle came back after your lunch with her. She was hopping mad. She kicked the Xerox machine." He looked at us as if that had some large significance.

Herb went on: "It was a new machine. It took weeks to get them to deliver it. You know how office supply people are."

"Then what happened?"

"She slammed the door of her office and locked it." Belle's office is the only one with a door to slam. And the only one with three windows.

"What time was that?" Alex asked.

"Just after three," Herb said. "I remember because we were supposed to have an edit meeting at three, and Belle was late. She canceled. All the editors were very upset. That was the third meeting in a row she'd canceled."

I asked, "Did she say anything to you? Receive any calls?"

Herb said, "She didn't do anything but growl at me when she walked by. Her calls were forwarded to Yolanda at the reception desk, but I don't think that will be much help. She's always hanging up on people and losing things."

I said, "About that poem you read at the will reading . . ."

"I did not write that poem," he stated. "And I have no idea who did. That's what I told the police, and that's what I'm telling you."

Herb paused. I took a moment to observe him. He was just two years older than me. Stylish short-back-and-sides brown hair, sweater vest. Crease in trousers. Not looking grieved in the slightest. Neither was Cheryl, for that matter. Herb hesitantly opened his mouth and then shut it. He nervously stroked a cucumber sculpture on his desk.

I said, "Come on, Herb. Spill it."

"Well, one tiny little thing did happen," he admitted. "A package came by bike messenger. Belle had me go out to get it at the reception desk. I was angry that she had me running errands, but her assistant was out sick, and I sit next closest to her. Or, rather, I sat next closest to her."

"What was the package?"

"I haven't told this to the police, Wanda. There didn't seem to be much point. I figured it was a prank from some lover of hers, or an especially enthused reader. But I guess you ought to know. I want to help you however I can."

I said, "Thanks a bunch."

He said, "The package was pretty big. A square box wrapped in brown paper." He made an outline with his hands. I'd say a twenty-inch square. "There was no return address, and no distinctive markings. I remember because the words 'Belle Beatrice care of *Midnight* Magazine' were the only writing on the package. I found that strange and took another look but didn't see anything else. The box was pretty light. I didn't think there was anything in it when I carried it into Belle's office. I put it down on her desk, and she started to open it. She didn't look very happy. I didn't know then she was having lunch with you, Wanda. I didn't know then that you were any part of her life, for that matter. Her eyes were all puffy—she must have been crying. She was depressed, certainly, but not too depressed to make a halfhearted come-on to me."

Alex said, "What did she say?"

Herb said, "Something like 'Thanks for getting the package. There must be some way to repay you.' You know, standard Belle stuff, but without the usual enthusiasm."

"She never let up, did she?" I commented.

"Don't think I'm not regretting my decision now," Herb said.

Alex said, "Um, the package?"

Herb went on: "So I put the package down on Belle's desk. She cut into the wrapping with an X-acto knife. The packing job was pretty good. Lots of layers of brown shipping paper. When she finished getting the paper off there was just a big white box. Then she looked up at me and shook the box. But there was no clear sound. It was definitely a mystery. Belle started to perk up. She loved surprises." I disagreed with that, but I let him go on. "She opened the box with her hands. When she got the top open a helium balloon rose up out of the box."

Alex said, "A balloon?"

Herb said, "Black party balloon full of helium. The sender had Liquid-Papered on the balloon the words 'Prick Me.' We saw that as it rose. She checked in the box for a card, but there was nothing else in there. The balloon was resting on the ceiling of her office. Belle stood on her chair with the X-acto knife in her hand. She got right under the balloon and punctured it."

Herb paused. He looked down at his hands. I said, "Go on."

"When the balloon popped, liquid flew all over the office. Most of it went on Belle and her desk. I got hit with some of it, too, but not much. A piece of paper also came down. It was drenched with the liquid, but we could make out the words 'I Came to Say Happy Birthday.' "

I said, "It was come?"

Herb said, "Diluted with water. Yes."

"You call a black balloon with exploding come one tiny little thing?" I asked.

Herb made the what-me-worry? gesture.

Alex said, "That's gross." Men always seem repelled by their own fluid.

Herb said, "I suppose it is kind of gross, but we get lots of weird mail working for a magazine like this."

I said, "Has anyone sent a come balloon before?"

Herb said, "Well, no. But I can't say that that was the grossest thing we've been sent."

"Then why don't you screen your mail?"

"I guess we never thought to do it. We like getting most of the weird stuff. Someone sent me this sculpture a while back." Herb gestured to the obscene cucumber thing.

"I've never seen a cucumber grow quite like that naturally," I said.

Alex asked, "Can we get a come sample?"

Herb said, "We cleaned it all up. Belle didn't want this to get out. She was very embarrassed. Wouldn't you be? When she realized she was covered in it, she screamed. We were locked in, and some people were standing outside banging on her office door. I told them we were okay and to go back to work. Belle waited until about seven to leave so no one would see her like that."

"Does Cheryl know about this?"

"Not that I know of."

Alex said, "Did you check the messenger service for a sender?"

"We asked Yolanda at the front desk. She said Stan, the guy who signs in messengers, just brought it up from the lobby himself. He didn't have a slip. Apparently someone just walked in and left it on his desk downstairs."

I said, "What about a description of the messenger?"

Herb said, "Yolanda said Stan didn't remember."

"Anything else? Did Belle mention any plans, places, people she was meeting later?"

Herb said, "She didn't really talk much after the incident. Just quietly sobbed."

Alex said, "So Belle died on her birthday, like Mark Twain." I wondered if he'd learned that fact on Channel 13.

Herb said, "Actually, Twain was born and died in a Halley's comet year." Alex frowned. He hates being shown up.

I said, "Whatever. Belle's birthday isn't for months. Whoever sent the balloon was wrong."

During my tenure at *Midnight* I hadn't been witness to any bizarre mailings. I was about to ask Herb more about these weird gifts, but he too loudly rustled some papers. A sign for us to go. We thanked Herb and left. He kissed me good-bye and whispered good luck. We stopped at Ginger's desk and left a note to call me at Do It Right.

We confirmed with Yolanda that she only remembered Stan bringing up the package without a slip. She said she wouldn't remember any messengers anyway, "So many come in and go out. I only remember the good-looking ones." We left her our number at the office. I made a mental note to get cards printed.

Our talk with Stan was as helpful. He said he'd gone to the bathroom and came back to find the package. He dutifully brought it up to Yolanda and forgot about it. I gave him my number and instructed him to call me immediately if anything like that happened again. He agreed. We stood in the lobby for a few hours and asked the people who came through if they had noticed a man carrying a big brown package into the building at five o'clock on Tuesday. Some people said they weren't sure. Most said they didn't remember. Alex and I went to Do It Right next to talk about Belle. Dead at thirty-five, recipient of exploding come balloons, an addicted flesh lover, a buyer of friends, a manipulator of colleagues, and a horribly confused woman up to her last hours. Hardly the picture of a rich, beautiful, internationally respected journalist.

This portrait doesn't much match the Belle I met at Dartmouth five years ago at my graduation. I saw her as a blond goddess devoid of faults, replete with all things charming and stunning. *Midnight* had just won the American Society of Magazine Editors' grand prize for general excellence after its first year out. The honor prompted the faculty of the college to award this distinguished alumna an honorary degree in fine arts. Belle Beatrice was a member of the first class of women admitted to Dartmouth in 1972, and a winner of seven A citations in her English major. She'd also won the English Department award for excellence in literary criticism in 1976, the year she graduated. Belle had been the first female editor of *The Dartmouth,* too, where I had just finished my reign as editorial page editor. A legend of sorts at the college, and certainly a legend in the incestuous publishing world in New York, Belle agreed to make an appearance at my graduation to receive her honorary degree. I was sitting close enough to the grandstand to see her clearly during the ceremony. I'd read *Midnight* all year long and was quite star-struck with her. She didn't speak when she accepted the degree. She only smiled and nodded to the college president. She was humble, generous, gracious, and—have I mentioned? —absolutely gorgeous.

I'd heard that Belle would be coming to *The Dartmouth*'s alumni party that night to tell a few real-world journalism stories. I abandoned my parents as soon as possible to dress for the party, intent on making my impression on the spectacular and brilliant Belle Beatrice. I don't think I wore makeup during my entire college career save for that night. Belle was perfection, keeping us enraptured for hours with her spurts of wisdom. Here are a few samples:

"An old friend once said to me, 'Belle, there are three kinds of people in this world. The all-lust people, the all-intellect, and the undecided. Which kind are you?' I stated proudly that I was all-lust but qualified that by saying I was born damn smart and could use my brain to promote my lustiness. He said he was all-lust, too. We confirmed our lustiness that afternoon, and afterward I decided he was born damn smart also. You see, the smartest people in this world are the ones who know when to let their bodies do the talking.

"Journalism has a built-in dementia to it. It is a jaded world—one that rewards cynicism and belittles naïveté. One learns fast to embrace the snappy retort and abandon sympathy for your colleagues as well as for the people who make the news. If you're not prepared to leave natural goody-goodiness behind, trade in your dreams now. Before you make a fool of yourself.

"My favorite months have always been June and October. June for the first waft of summer—my favorite season. The heat is what turns me on. Fall is the most literary season. Read the nineteenth-century women novelists; their stories are all set in autumn.

"What do I think about the feminist movement? Forgive me, but that is a ridiculously passé question. At *Midnight* we know we're women, and we know what to expect. Maybe we know not to expect the best. That's what keeps us fresh and watchful. We see what's running up our asses. You can only stay ahead if you know what's behind you."

"I got my start as a hatcheck girl at a Mafia nightclub writing book reviews for an underground newspaper that couldn't afford to pay me. Then I got a staff job at that paper as a copy editor. Of course, I was a terrible copy editor. Too big for my shackles. I've always had trouble with the notion of paying dues. If you're an exceptional person, capable of great things, why waste time shoveling the bullshit? But I advise you young people to suck it up. It isn't so bad. It depends what you're sucking."

My only chance to speak to her privately was when she finally went to the bathroom after countless beers. (Strange—our first meeting in a bathroom, and our last words in one.) I gushed to her shamelessly while she washed her hands. I told her thirty-seven times how much I respected her and that I wanted to be just like her. She smiled patiently and gave me her card. She told me to call her when I got to New York.

My parents lived in Short Hills, New Jersey, at the time—a rich suburb thirty minutes outside the city. The first business day after I returned from Dartmouth I called Belle. She didn't remember me. I reminded her who I was. She told me to come see her at the magazine, which I did that afternoon. She offered me a job on the spot to be her assistant, something I later learned was unheard of. A week later I had moved from Short Hills to Brooklyn. And you know the rest. I'm not so green anymore. Those were my salad days; these are my hard-boiled days. I seem to be moving up the food chain. Red meat can't be far away.

Back from *Midnight,* Alex and I found the Do It Right door open. I was too preoccupied to care. I was thinking about two hands around Belle's neck. She must have been terrified. Gasping for air, fighting, and afraid to die. I shuddered. Another huge pang of missing her hit me as we walked into the office. I didn't have a chance to think about her, though. My favorite public dicks were inside waiting—Dick O'Flanahey and Bucky. Dick sat behind my desk, stuffing a Twinkie under his mustache. Bucky leaned against the file cabinet he'd previously violated, picking his back molars with a paper clip. The file on Johann was spread out on my desk, wads of Twinkie cream spotting the loose papers. I strode over, flicked the blobs off, and reclaimed the file. I held it tightly to my chest. (So I forgot to hide the file. So I can be an idiot.)

Dick said, "It's all yours, cupcake. We've seen it all."

Bucky, as gravely as he could, said, "Withholding evidence in a murder investigation is a felony offense."

Dick said, "At this point, cupcake, we can take you downtown and book you. But we can also make this easy for you. If you cooperate with us, answer all our questions, and keep us abreast of your investigation, we won't put you away. Call it a threat if you want, I don't give a shit. Tell me everyone you've spoken to today, and all non-entry information on Johann Pesto."

I said, "I don't have anything."

Bucky opened his cavernous mouth to speak, but Dick held his hand up to stop him. He said, "Let me remind you who is wearing the badge in this room. Detective Squirely and myself. No one else. We are the cops. You are a private citizen. Our days are filled by protecting you people. And what do we get in return? We're called pigs by ten-year-olds. We get shot at. We never see our families, if we ever had time to get them. We never sleep. We eat doughnuts and Twinkies and drink so much coffee we all have ulcers. We get called away from ballgames, movies, sex. But all that doesn't mean anything to us. You know why? Because there is something in us that wants to keep the city safe from men who like to put their hands around women's necks and squeeze the life from them. So go ahead and hate me. But we have a job to do. Even if we, the badged ones, don't have half a mil as incentive, it is still our obligation to solve this murder. Not to mention how crappy the police department would look if you took home your little doggie bag from the Beatrice estate and we turn up squat." Dick paused. He took a deep breath. He said, "Now, sweetie. All persons involved with Mr. Pesto are involved in this case. That means you, Wanda Mallory, private *citizen.* Now that we're all clear, I want a precise description of Johann's movements from the day he met Belle on. Your write-up in there sucks." He pointed at the file in my arms.

If he was trying to make me feel sorry for him, it wasn't working. I said, "I don't remember."

Bucky said, "It's your job to remember."

Dick snarled, "Shut up. I'm handling this."

I said, "Look, gentlemen, I'm not up to this right now. Someone close to me just died. Don't let the door hit you on the butt on the way out."

"We're not going anywhere until you tell us about Johann, and Herb Stoltz, too, for that matter."

I was losing my patience. "Herb? Don't tell me he's a suspect."

Dick said, "You must not know him as well as you think you do."

I said, "Enough shoptalk. Just get the fuck out, or—"

Dick said, "Or what, cupcake? Is he going to beat the crap out of us?" He pointed to Alex, who didn't seem pleased. Dick laughed, bits of golden sponge cake stuck in his teeth. Bucky walked over to Alex and gently felt his wiry bicep with thumb and forefinger. Alex reacted by tightening his fists.

"Don't get all jumpy now," Bucky yukked.

Dick said, "Don't worry about that beanpole. He couldn't hit the side of a barn with those fists." Alex looked at me. He was losing his good humor. Dick said, "Don't go looking to her for help. The only help she can get is the fashion police." He stepped over the line on that one.

Dick rose from my chair. He said, "Last chance, sweetie. Tell me about Johann. *Now.*" I said nothing.

He said, "I can see that you're not respecting the badge, cupcake. Things could get ugly." He took a step toward me.

Alex said, "You move one step closer to her, I promise you will be sorry." Alex cocked my (empty) standing ashtray, threatening to wheelhouse Dick. Bucky rolled his eyes at the dramatics. For a moment I let myself revel in the tension in the room.

My office phone rang. I let it. The machine would pick up; I didn't want to disrupt the afternoon entertainment. A woman's voice came over the box: "Wanda Mallory. We met last night. I have reason to fear for my life, and I need your help. You know where to find me. I think we can arrange a deal." Then she hung up. Dick and Bucky heard the whole thing. Dick twirled his mustache in silence for a moment and then made a dash for my desk to get the tape. Alex tripped him with the ashtray. He fell to the orange carpet.

I popped the tape and threw it out the window. Bucky ran out of the office for the street, and Dick—in a crawl position displaying haunches like a Great Dane—followed him out. I looked out the window and watched a homeless person pick up the tape, fit it into one of the pockets of his overcoat, and walk down the block. By the time Bucky got to the spot there was no tape. Dick, stumbling, joined him. Alex and I snickered as they scoured the street like ants in search of a french fry. Nothing lasts for long in the Times Square black hole.

"Am I too excitable?" Alex asked.

I said, "The ashtray was a bit much."

Alex sat down in the client comfy chair and grinned shyly. I sat down behind my desk and smiled back, showing all my teeth. I found a replacement tape in my desk and put it in the machine.

Martha was the caller. I didn't need to listen twice. It was four o'clock on Friday. The public dicks would be frantic looking for a connection. We had to get to her first.

CHAPTER FIVE

THE FRUITS OF DIPLOMACY

"I don't believe I'm familiar with you." Mr. Gladman extended his hand to Alex.

"Alex Beaudine, sir. Pleased to meet you." Alex shook Gladman's hand.

Gladman said, "Very pleased to meet you. And Ms. Mallory. A delight to see you. You're looking fine, I might add. Plump as a Jersey tomato." He cleaned his Coke-bottle specs and saw I wasn't taking his compliment well. He continued, "Please, sit." It was 4:30 on Friday afternoon.

His office looked the same as before, only bigger with fewer people. Gladman looked the same. The same greased Grecian Formula brown hair and a dapper tweed three-piece with a watch chain extending to his vest pocket. We sat on the edges of the overstuffed French provincial chairs across from his desk and smiled at him. He smiled back at us. He said, "We all seem to be in a pleasant humor today.

Splendid. How's the investigation going? Only a few days left, I guess."

I asked, "What's that?"

"I said, 'How's the investigation?'"

I said, "I got that. What confused me was what sounded like 'only a few days left.'"

He said, "It's Friday, and the murder occurred on Monday night."

"Yes, but we didn't know about the deadline until Thursday morning."

Gladman said, "I apologize for the confusion, but Belle Beatrice's will states that you have one week to solve this unnatural death. I wasn't sure if that meant seven days after the murder or seven days after the will reading. I've had a few of my colleagues look at the will, and the decision was unanimous. We all agree that you have seven days after the *murder* to solve the crime. I know that only gives you three and a half days, but I'm sure you're right in the thick of things and that you've nearly got this thing wrapped up already." He cocked an eyebrow at us.

I said, "Hold your water, Mr. Gladman. How could I know that there was any money at stake until I heard the will?"

Gladman said, "Be glad that you heard the will only two days after the murder."

Alex said, "Excuse me, sir, but don't you think you should have cleared this up on Tuesday?"

Gladman said, "The wheels of justice turn slowly, Mr. Beaudine, but the law is the law. I apologize, Ms. Mallory, and I assure you that if I could have anticipated Belle being killed, I would have checked this out beforehand."

"Not good enough," I said. I was furious.

"If that's how you feel, you can forfeit your claim to the bequest right now, and I can arrange for the moneys to be divided between the New York Public Library and the Historical Society today."

I said, "You so much as pick up that phone and I'll tear your arm off."

He arched an eyebrow at me. This wasn't going well. He reached for the phone.

Alex said, "I've got a better idea. Why don't we try and compromise? Wanda has important friends at the newspapers and magazines around town who could interpret this stipulation as a tad unreasonable. I don't know how well BG&B would come off if there were a few well-placed editorials in those publications, but I'm sure there are a ton of lawyerly types running around this building who can see clear to giving us one more day. The murder took place on Monday, the will reading on Thursday. So what about giving us until, say, midnight on Tuesday? Sound fair to everyone?"

Gladman scowled at him. I said, "I wonder if Pete Hamill at the *Post* is busy for lunch tomorrow. He was a close friend of Belle's and all. May I use your phone?"

He said, "Will you excuse me for a moment?" We nodded, and he ran out of the office. I got up and opened the wood panel door in back—the door Martha had come through after the will reading. She wasn't there. I turned back to Alex. He was flipping through Gladman's Rolodex.

"She's not here."

"Aren't you going to thank me?" Alex asked.

"Let's see what Gladman says when he comes back." I didn't really know Pete Hamill, or anyone else in publishing that could do any damage to a law firm with BG&B's reputation.

Alex said, "What's Martha's last name?"

I shrugged. I went into her office and poked around in her desk. There was a file marked "personal" in the bottom drawer. It contained her health insurance forms and her pay stubs. I swiped a stub and returned to my French provincial seconds before Gladman came through the office door. He sat down in a resigned fashion.

Gladman said, "So next Tuesday by midnight should be the accurate deadline. Oh—deadline. Isn't that a horrifying choice of word?" Gladman laughed and bobbed his head. He stopped with an abrupt hand clap. "If that's all, I really must be off. I've got a dinner appointment."

I said, "Mr. Gladman, is Martha available for a few minutes? I need to talk to her for a second."

He said, "Why on earth would you want to talk to my assistant?"

I said, "This may sound silly, sir, but I couldn't help admiring the shoes she wore at the will reading. I wanted to ask where she got them." (Actually, I had noticed her shoes; they were black and red Susan Bennis/Warren Edwards.)

"She called in sick this morning. Sinus problems."

"I see. Well, would you have her call me if you hear from her?"

"Yes, yes. Now I must be going."

He scooted us toward the larger door of his office,

the one that led out to the hall. He locked that door and led us through the glass doors by the reception desk. He instructed Emily, the receptionist, to take all calls. We left the BG&B building together. Needless to say, I was upset about losing a day and a half like that.

On the street I showed Alex the pay stub. It had her full name—Martha Schpreckenspiel. We searched for a working pay phone for five blocks. Finally we found one and called information. Martha's address was 123 East 31st Street. I wasn't surprised. That's Johann's building.

We didn't bother calling her. If she was home, she probably wouldn't answer the phone. Plus, she said we should find her. We jumped in a cab and rode over. There was traffic as usual in midtown. Cab fares had been my biggest expense so far during the investigation. I'd been keeping all the receipts for tax purposes.

We finally pulled up just before 5:00. Martha and Johann's building was art deco with a small geometric glass-and-ironwork facade. Probably twenty apartments total. We checked the buzzer board. Johann and Martha lived on the same floor. That could be how they'd met. We buzzed her apartment. Number 5E: no answer. We buzzed Johann at 5B. No answer. I pressed every button on the board. Finally a woman answered.

"Who is it?"

Alex said, "Pest control."

"Go to hell. Pest control came last week."

"We missed a few apartments."

"I know your kind. Buzz every apartment until someone lets you in and then you rob us blind and rape us, satisfying your maniacal anger toward your mother. Go to hell."

Our next move: wait and watch from the coffee shop across the street. It wouldn't be easy. The sun was setting, and the streetlight on the corner was broken. There was a fluorescent light in the lobby of Martha's building, but the tube was nearly burned out. We sat on stools at the counter, waited, and watched. This is the boring part of detective work. It requires nothing but patience—something I haven't got a lot of.

Stephanopoulos's Coffee House bustled with after-work baklava heads. The grill man yammered in Greek over the sizzle of cheeseburgers. Alex ordered coffee, and I watched in horror as he downed one cup and asked for a refill. I had a Diet Coke. I asked Alex to call the machine at Do It Right and check for messages; I didn't want to leave my post by the window and miss something. Alex came back with two messages. One from Santina, asking us to dinner. The other from Skip Giddy, asking about my *Shinola* article, and for my company that evening. Alex said, "You sure are in demand."

I said, "We probably won't make it to Santi's. We could use the free meal."

Alex said, "So, you've been seeing *Skip* again." He said the name with obvious disdain. Alex and I had just started to be friends when Skip broke my heart. Alex had had to do a lot of consoling. They'd only met once, when we bumped into Skip on his street in SoHo. That was during my Skip-obsessed days. I walked past his building every night at 6:30, hoping

I'd catch him coming home from work. The one night I did catch him, I was with Alex. "How're you doing?" conversations turn my insides to orange marmalade. The memory made my Diet Coke taste funny.

I said, "He only wants the Belle story."

"I bet," Alex replied. He sipped his coffee. "Do I have to remind you what he did to you?"

"That was a year ago. And he just wants the story."

"Are you going to do it?"

"Depends if I'll have to."

"You know, Wanda, you don't have to do anything for him," Alex said.

"What do you mean by that?"

"I mean you don't have to *do* anything for him."

"Is it possible that I'm doing something for myself?" I asked.

"I didn't know you needed to get laid so badly."

"When and whom I lay are not your business."

"You made it my business when I had to put you back together last year when he dumped you."

I said, "I know what I'm doing."

He said, "I don't doubt that. You know how to set yourself up for assholes like him really well."

I was getting pissed off. I said, "I'm different now."

He said, "And he's changed, too, I'm sure."

"Back off, Alex."

"I bet he wants to marry you now."

"You're pushing me."

"What makes you think you're different from the thousands of other women he's fucked?"

I slapped Alex in the face. It felt swell. He'd crossed the line. I knew he wouldn't hit me back; I was wearing my glasses. He said, "*I* know you're different from the thousands of other women he's fucked, but I doubt *he* does." I slapped him again. He said, "You can hit me all you want. But that doesn't change the kind of sleazebag Skip is, and the disgusting position you put yourself in whenever he fucks you."

I raised my hand again, but he caught me by the wrist. He looked me in the eye and said, "I've given up trying to figure out what you want from men. Most of the time I think you don't want anything. But then you go crazy for a shithead like Skip, and I'm convinced you're a masochist. What is it about him?"

It might have something to do with multiple orgasm, I thought. I said, "If this isn't the swamp rat calling the kettle slimy."

"Let's just say I'm more discriminating than you." He released my wrist, and I straightened up on my stool.

"I can see how proud you are of that girlfriend no one's ever met."

"What girlfriend?" he asked.

"The one you spend all your nights with."

"I spend all my nights in the darkroom at Chelsea Developers."

I said, "Whatever." The darkroom—an unlikely euphemism.

He looked away and said, "I'm sorry. I'll stay out of your personal life."

I said, "Likewise." I sipped my Diet Coke through the straw, watching it gurgle back down and then fizz to the top. I asked, "Does your cheek hurt?"

"Yes."

"Good." We stayed in Stephanopoulos's until 9:30 P.M. We ate dinner. Alex got a turkey club on white toast, hold the mayo. I got a tuna melt on rye, extra coleslaw.

Alex and I don't have the perfect friendship. In this business perfect friendships don't exist. It has something to do with knowing not to trust anyone. The story of our first case together might help explain. When I first started working at Binkerton it was run by a salty old man named Benzi Lewis. In his heyday he'd worked homicide for the New York City Police Department. He was also Alex's uncle. Alex didn't work at Binkerton at the time; he shot fashion spreads for women's magazines. Benzi was kind enough to hire me as a receptionist within days of my leaving *Midnight.* He was a pleasant man with a wiry white beard—not the kind of man one might think of as a detective who'd killed two dozen men in his thirty-year career. Rather, the kind you envision with a parakeet on his shoulder.

I typed, made phone calls, got Benzi's lunch, and did background research at the library. Benzi always said I was smart enough to be a detective. And then one day he let me tail Sukie Wilshire. Her pit bull of a husband suspected her of having an affair. When Benzi was arranging the contract Sebastian Wilshire insisted that we get pictures of his wife in bed with her lover. No other information interested him. Benzi suggested his nephew, Alex Beaudine, fashion photographer, to shoot the lady, but Wilshire insisted we use Charles Leggy, the man who had taken pictures at his daughter's wedding. Apparently the pictures were choice.

Leggy turned out to be British and suitably pompous. He glided into Binkerton carrying a 24″ x 36″ leather portfolio full of wedding and bar mitzvah pictures. I told him that he'd be chasing after a wayward wife with me, on call twenty-four hours a day. I quoted a fee, and he promptly zipped up his side of beef and made for the door.

I ran to stop him. "Mr. Wilshire insisted we use you. You took some wedding pictures for him?"

"Did you say Mr. Sebastian Wilshire, the wire hanger king?"

"I guess."

Leggy said, "Right then, madam. When do we start?"

Over the next couple of weeks Leggy and I were on Sukie Wilshire's heels like toilet paper. It was my first case, and I was determined to get my man. We watched her go to the market, shop on Fifth Avenue, speak at a Junior League luncheon. We sat through at least twenty movies with her (client expenses). The worst part of the case was, without question, the time spent with Leggy and his fetid pipe. I came to loathe Mr. Wilshire, too. He checked in four times a day, barking orders. He was a paranoid control freak, insisting that I never call him. (He suspected the paramour to be his partner at the wire hanger plant.) Eventually, with perpetual garlic breath after one too many falafel lunches in Central Park watching Sukie feed pigeons, I got to thinking. Why *wasn't* she having an affair? All she did was moon around.

Leggy and I came up with squat. I called Wilshire in to Binkerton to admit defeat—no need to mention the paralyzing effect on my ego. I described Sukie's impossibly tedious activities, and pit-bull Wilshire said, "These are subtleties. I want answers." His frothing jowls dried up a bit when he looked over Leggy's contact sheets of Sukie eating arugula and chèvre salads at Raoul's, buying popcorn in movie theaters, feeding the pigeons in the park.

He put the sheets down and quietly said, "How much am I paying you?" I quoted a fee. "Did I pay for these pictures?" he asked.

"Every blessed one," I said.

"Can I get prints? Sukie looks lovely in a few."

"I'll have Leggy get on it right away."

He wrote a check and politely thanked me for my time. He paused at the door and adjusted his lapels. Then he walked out, splintered like a broken bat. The change in Wilshire was what got to me. I'd seen clients' temper flares before, but never had I seen a pit bull transform into a Lhasa apso pup so quickly. He was in love with his wife. It was touching. I called Leggy and told him to make prints for Wilshire. When he asked if he could come pick up his money, I told him, "The check's in the mail, and I won't come in your mouth." He didn't get it.

I sat around Binkerton until Benzi got back from his day in the field. I told him what had happened. Benzi said, "Give it one more try. Have Alex Beaudine go with you tonight." That was Benzi's motto. One more try. I didn't have any plans, so I called Alex, and we went over to the Wilshire residence at 78th and Park, right by the Louis Argola Salon, where Santi does the beauty thing. Alex and I connected immediately. We were as green as hell, but before the night was over we got the shot. The next day I called Wilshire back to Binkerton. Alex and I greeted him with smiles.

Wilshire said, "What is this? Am I expected to give you more money? And I told you never to call me at Hangers R Us."

I said, "Will you take a look at these contact sheets, sir?" Alex and I had stayed up all night developing in his darkroom.

He barked, "I saw enough prints yesterday. Will you please get on with this?"

I said, "All right, sir. After you left yesterday I was moved. I decided to spend one more night on the case. I waited at your building with Alex Beaudine, my photographer."

Alex said, "Hello."

I said, "Your wife left the building at 10:29 P.M. Were you there, sir?"

"No, I was not there," he snarled.

"Where were you?"

"I met a friend for dinner."

"What time did you return home?"

"I didn't return home last night."

Alex said, "Do you often spend the night away from home?"

He snapped, "I don't see what business that is of yours."

I said, "I'm sorry, sir. May I continue?" He nodded. "Your doorman hailed your wife a cab. We followed her via cab to 356 Chambers Street. The building appeared to be abandoned, but a quick check at City Hall confirmed that there are five loft spaces leased out. The spaces are used for parties mainly, according to the landlord."

Alex said, "We went to see him this morning. He recognized a picture of your wife and said she is one of his renters."

I said, "He knew her as Gertrude Babbles. Are you familiar with that address, sir?"

I could see the transformation to Lhasa apso beginning. He said, "No, I'm not."

"Alex took these pictures of Sukie entering the building on Chambers Street. Is that her, sir?"

"Yes."

"She entered the building at 11:06 P.M. We saw a light go on on the second floor. These pictures were taken at 11:30 of a man in a red scarf entering the building. Alex climbed the fire escape of the building across the street. With his telephoto lens he got these pictures. Is that your wife?"

"Yes," Wilshire said. "I recognize the mole." He was absorbed in the pictures. Nothing too raunchy; missionary position. *Midnight*-level bobbing butt shots. But, unquestionably, Sukie bonking another man.

Wilshire said, "I can't see his face."

I continued, "Three and a half hours later Sukie left the building. Ten minutes after that the man left. You can see his face better in these shots. He couldn't pull his scarf up because of the pipe."

Wilshire paled. "Leggy."

I said, "Otherwise known as Sebastian Babbles, according to the landlord."

Wilshire said, "He's taken pictures of me and my mistress. We had an arrangement."

I said, "I take it you didn't know the arrangement included boffing your wife."

He said, "Don't be flip, girlie."

I said, "I took the liberty of sending Leggy these choice shots. I hope you don't mind."

Wilshire smiled for the first time in our acquaintance. He said, "Not at all." He wrote a tremendous check to Binkerton. And I got my first dose of victory.

Alex had so much fun climbing the fire escape that he decided to stay at the agency part-time. Not as a photographer, but as a detective second class. Alex and I worked together from then on. I was promoted to full detective. Benzi dropped dead of a heart attack shortly after, and all his staff quit. I moved to my Times Square office, and with the money from my grandmother's Picasso I started Do It Right. Alex agreed to keep working part-time for me. I tried to seduce Benzi's regular clients to come to Do It Right. None did. We almost tossed in the washcloth, but it was around that time that Belle sought me out. She became our number-one client. With her dead, we could lose it all again.

My loyalties are few but fierce. I know I'm not too good at showing them. But I am loyal to Alex and to Do It Right—not necessarily in that order.

Before Alex and I left Stephanopoulos's I asked the cashier if he'd noticed a tall, very attractive woman with long brown hair leaving the building across the street that afternoon. He said, "Sure, lady. I see her all the time."

I said, "Did you see her today?"

He ran his hands through his hair, wiped off the grease on his spotty apron, and said, "I don't know. Maybe today."

Alex asked, "What time?"

He turned to me and said, "What's your name? I never see you before." He smiled. His front tooth was chipped.

I said, "Wanda Mallory."

"I am Cosmos. What you doing tonight? You want to go dancing with me? We have a good time."

"That's very sweet, but I think my boyfriend here would mind."

Cosmos said to Alex, "You a very lucky man."

Alex said, "I know."

He said, "Okay. I tell you. The woman left with a man."

"Big guy? Blond? Long hair?" I asked.

He said, "I don't remember." He would have recognized Johann, I thought.

Alex asked, "Do you remember what he was wearing?"

"No."

"Anything about him?"

"No."

"And what time was that?" Alex asked.

"Right before my shift."

"Can you be more specific?" I asked.

"Before noon."

I said, "Thank you, Cosmos. You've been a big help."

"You ever break up, you come see me. We go dancing, okay?"

I said, "You bet."

Alex and I walked over the dozen-odd blocks south and west to Times Square. It was warm, even with the sun down. I worked up a slight sweat. Alex didn't; he's in better shape. The neon spun and blinked—TDK, Maxell. Info rotated around the zipper on the *Newsday* building—five youths in Queens beat a policeman to death . . . Mets nuke Oakland in Series 14-2 . . . Pick 6 jackpot $2,000,000. People pushed in and out of the two movie theaters on the corner. A hot dog man wheeled his cart against the light and almost got hit. A born-again with a Fender amp was threatening the throngs for not believing Jesus to be the messiah. It was just before ten o'clock. Alex and I walked up the four flights to the Do It Right office.

The door was open. I didn't know whom to expect; probably the public dicks were at it again. We walked in. Johann Pesto was sitting behind my desk flicking my table lighter on and off.

I said, "Alex, meet Johann Pesto."

Alex said, "I've heard a lot about you."

"You've probably read about me, too," Johann said.

"Do you mind?" I waved him away from my desk. He stood and watched me take my seat. It always feels better to be the one behind the desk. I said, "What can we do for you?"

He said, "I want you to come with me."

Alex said, "She's not going anywhere without me."

"Fine, then. You both come. Martha's waiting."

"Where is she, Johann?" I asked.

He said, "My apartment."

We took the elevator down to the street (it only works going down) and hopped a cab back to 31st Street. I had seen the message light blinking on my machine but decided it could wait.

Martha looked lovely in yet another red dress. "Is that a Marc Jacobs?" I asked. Alex was staring at her.

She smiled. "I waited for you all afternoon." She was sitting on the yellow modular couch. The whole one-bedroom apartment was yellow. Very thematic. She suggested we sit in the yellow-canvas director's chairs at the amoeba-shaped coffee table and make ourselves comfortable.

I said, "We looked for you at BG&B, and we waited at the coffee shop across the street for hours. Where the hell were you?"

"The Orchid Lounge. I just got back." Of course. I should have known she'd be there—the one place we had in common that was completely secret.

I said, "Sorry, I didn't think of it." So I can be an idiot.

Martha said, "I want to show you something." She pulled back the collar of her dress to reveal a bruised neck. Clearly a strangulation attempt.

Alex said, "Just like Belle." He has an unusual talent for stating the obvious.

I took my steno out of my bag. I bit off the pen cap. "Okay. From the beginning."

Johann was across the room leaning on the yellow-painted bureau. "Just for the record," he said, "I want to say that I do not like the way you set us up the other night."

I said, "I didn't set you up. I just played along. Besides, I don't think you're in any position to complain." He seemed to forget his suspecthood.

Martha said, "Honey, she might be able to help us. You should apologize."

Johann whined, "I don't want to," confirming my theory that most men are children.

Alex said, "Enough of this. Who attacked you?"

Martha leaned forward on the couch. "I don't know."

"Any guesses?" I asked.

"No particular guesses, but I think it was probably the man who's been sending me the letters."

I said, "Back up. First tell me about the attack."

"It was horrible." She shook a little—a nice dramatic touch, I thought. "I was walking home from work. Mr. Gladman and I had to stay late Thursday night working. I think I finally left around nine o'clock. It had gotten dark already, but I wasn't worried. It's only twenty-odd blocks home, and I've never run into trouble before. At the corner, right up here on Park Avenue, I thought I saw a man hiding in a doorway. I sped up my pace. When I turned the corner onto 31st Street he was on me. He grabbed me from behind and put his hands around my neck. I had trouble breathing, and my life flashed before my eyes. It sounds corny, but it really happened." She widened her eyes by way of confirmation. Again, the dramatic shake.

Johann walked over and sat next to her on the couch. He put his arm around her. I wondered if they'd choreographed this scene. He said, "Thank God I was out on our fire escape having a Dunhill. I saw the whole attack. I ran downstairs and up the street. The attacker saw me coming and vanished. I know I should have gone after him, but I had to help Martha. She was lying on the sidewalk, fighting for breath." They looked at each other and embraced. "I can't tell you how glad we are I didn't quit smoking," he added.

I said, "On that touching note, I'm sure you won't mind if I light up." I already had the cigarette in my mouth. I struck a match, inhaled, and exhaled. "Description of the guy?"

Martha said, "He came at me from behind."

"What about when you saw him lurking ominously in the shadows?"

"It was too dark. Except he was wearing a hat. A big hat. With a brim."

"Johann? Description?" I asked.

He said, "I just saw the struggle. By the time I got close enough, he was gone. I do remember a hat, though." They nodded at me in unison. I looked at Alex. He gave me the run-with-it-babe look.

"Did you report the attack to the police?"

"No," Martha said. "We agreed to call you instead."

"Why?"

"Because we think my strangler killed Belle. We wanted to help in your investigation."

And help clear Johann as a suspect. Quid pro quo

action. I said, "So why did you wait so long to contact me?"

Johann said, "I made her wait. I didn't like the idea of calling you in the first place. Just for the record, Martha wanted to call right after it happened."

A thought occurred to me. "Why don't you have a Swedish accent?" I asked. "And why do you keep saying 'for the record'?"

"My parents sent me to an American school in Stockholm. And," he smiled to himself, "I picked up that phrase from Belle."

I sucked on my cigarette, pondering Johann's relationship with Belle. *Could* he have killed her? Everyone seemed to be waiting for me to speak. I said, finally, "Ashtray?"

Martha said, "Johann, isn't there one in the kitchen sink?"

He rose to fetch it. Alex stopped him and volunteered. He asked Martha if it was okay to get himself some water; she said sure.

"You a heavy smoker, Johann?" I asked.

"Some days."

"Funny thing your not having an ashtray on your coffee table."

He said, "Martha doesn't like the smoke, so I usually go on the fire escape. Look, what is this? I don't have to justify my smoking habits to you."

I said, "No, you don't." Alex came back with a dirty ashtray and a big glass of water.

He leaned toward my ear and said, "Can I talk to you in the kitchen?" I looked at him, annoyed at his interrupting my investigation, but his eyes promised pay dirt. I asked Martha if I could confer with my partner for a few seconds in the other room. She said sure.

Alex led me straight to the fridge. He opened the door and exhibited the twenty-odd Tupperware containers full of a milky liquid. I said, "Is that what I think it is?"

He said, "I do believe so."

"Are you thinking what I'm thinking?"

"If you're thinking about being in bed together, then we are." He winked. I rabbit-punched him lightly in the stomach.

I said, "Then we're not." We returned to the other room.

Martha and Johann were huddled together on the couch. They broke apart and looked at me expectantly.

I said, "I've had an easier time swallowing raw liver than your story."

Johann jumped up and said, "You see now, Martha? This woman can't be trusted."

She said, "But you haven't heard the whole story. I mentioned the letters before—"

Alex said, "Letters from the attacker."

She said, "I assume they're from the attacker."

"Threatening letters?" I asked.

"They're poems, actually. No signature. Typewritten," she said.

I said, "Show me." Johann reached into the folds of the modular couch. He pulled out a manila envelope and handed it to me. There were a few dozen poems in it. I read a few out loud:

Ode to Martha's Lips

Your lips are like plump raspberries
glistening with juice,
Squashed by my gigantic schlong
all over your face.
They part, they speak,
they house your vinelike tongue,
winding around my splendiferous member
like a golden retriever in heat
grasping my willing leg.

Ode to Martha's Eyes

Her wine grapes see out, but not through.
If they did, they'd see the other man.
The hot-lust king, boiling, consuming,
waiting for come-hither glances
from your useless eyes.

Ode to Martha's Ankles

I watch the celery stalks of my beloved's ankles
like I await high tide,
to be drowned, washed away
like broken wreckage from a lumbering heap.
Perfectly symmetrical and dimpled,
my beloved's ankles.
It is difficult to imagine the physics—
how such delicate stems support
such weighty gams.

Johann said, "Martha hates that part about her weighty gams, don't you, honey?" Martha flushed.

I said, "I would, too."

"And look," Johann said, pointing at Martha's body. "She doesn't have weighty gams at all. Her legs are thin."

I said, "I can only imagine how this poet would describe me."

"From a literary standpoint, I'd say these poems suck," Alex commented.

I flipped through the pile—standard white Eaton typing paper. I said, "There seems to be a poem for nearly every body part. Here's 'Ode to Martha's Caboose.' "

Johann said, "The poems started arriving on Tuesday, after Belle's murder. That guy read a poem like these at the funeral. I described him to Martha, and she says he matches the body type of the strangler."

"Herb Stoltz is no murderer," I said.

Johann asked, "How can you be sure?"

"Good point, Wanda," Alex agreed.

My cigarette had burned out in my fingers. I dropped the singed filter in the ashtray. I said, "Martha, you were obviously aware that Johann was sleeping with Belle. Right?"

"Yes." She dropped her eyes.

"Considering how cuddly-wuddly the two of you are tonight, I can't see why you would put up with that."

"Johann is free to experiment sexually. As I am." That might explain the Orchid Lounge incident, but not a full-fledged affair that included a marriage proposal. Martha shifted slightly away from him, but not for effect. Johann's jaw tightened. She wasn't telling the whole truth.

Alex said, "Sexual freedom is out, don't you know?"

"I met Belle before Martha and I knew how much we meant to each other. I was trying to break it off with Belle," Johann explained.

"So that's why you proposed to her the night before her murder?"

"No, I—"

"Would trying to break it off include murder?"

"I don't have to justify myself to you."

"You'll have to justify some things to someone, Johann. Or, to put it bluntly, you are fucked," I said. "Why are these poems in your apartment and not Martha's? Weren't they sent to her?"

Martha said, "I'm here most of the time."

Alex leaned forward in his chair. "And just out of curiosity, why are there twenty plastic containers full of come in the fridge?"

Martha thought quickly. You could practically see the light bulbs flashing behind her eyes. She said, "I use it for facial cream. It's full of protein, you see. It keeps my complexion clear." She smiled to herself—well done. I'd read about Swedish women doing that in *Cosmo.* She could have picked up the practice from Johann. She turned to me and said, "You really should try it."

"I just might," I said. "Any witnesses to the attack?"

Johann said, "There wasn't anyone nearby. And you know how New Yorkers are about keeping to themselves."

"Conveniently so." I stood and shoved the steno and pen back in my purse. I said, "I'm tired. I want to go home and play cigarette-pack hockey with my cat. I'll be talking to you."

Alex said, "One last thing—where were you between ten and midnight the night of the murder?" He gave me the eye. He's always wanted to say that.

Johann spoke for them both. "We were here together. No phone calls or visitors, unfortunately." With that, Alex and I made for the door and waved goodbye.

Once outside Alex said, "They could be telling the truth, you know." We checked and saw the fire escape *did* hang over 31st Street, and the streetlight *was* burned out. At least they got that right. I decided we should go see our friend Cosmos again and ask him if he saw the alleged attack on Thursday night.

Upon entering, the restaurant had the familiar pleasant/unpleasant smell of grease and smoke. There were only two customers at the counter. Alex said he had to make a phone call. Reporting in to his woman, no doubt. I walked to the counter.

Cosmos didn't recognize me immediately. I was practically in his lap when he said, "You come to go dancing!"

I said, "No, Cosmos. I want you ask you some questions. Were you working last night at nine o'clock?"

He said, "I get off in a half hour. You sit. Have coffee. We have a good time. What you like? Some homemade pie?"

"Did you see anything unusual? A mugging maybe?"

"Yes, something. I don't remember. Okay? You sit."

"Come on, Cosmos. Last night. Right on the corner." But he had gone down the counter to get coffee for me. I remained standing. He put the mug in front of me. He smiled. He poked his tongue under his chipped tooth.

He said, "You sit. Half hour, we go dancing."

I said, "Look, Cosmos, I don't want to go dancing with you. I only want information. Now tell me what you saw."

Cosmos reached out and caressed one of my red locks. He said, "You're a natural woman. Look at the hair on your arms. Natural woman. I like you. You're very pretty." I pushed his hand away, and he accidentally pulled my hair. He said, "I'm sorry, lady. We save touching for later. After we go dancing. Just a taste now, okay?" He kissed my hand.

I'd had enough. I pulled out Mama. Legs spread wide, I held the gun with both hands and pointed it in Cosmos's face. A woman at the counter screamed, and the other patron fell to the floor. Cosmos froze. I said, "Describe what you saw or you'll never go dancing again."

He stared, transfixed by the gun, and rambled hysterically in Greek. I turned to the woman who had screamed and pointed Mama at her. "Tell me what he said!" I yelled.

She said, "He says he wasn't wearing his glasses and couldn't see that far away. He says he takes off his glasses when pretty women come into the restaurant." I pointed the gun back at Cosmos. How could I blame him? I do the same thing. I lowered the gun and wrote my name and phone number on a napkin. I shoved the paper in Cosmos's apron pocket and said, "You remember anything, give me a call." I turned to go and heard a crash. Cosmos had fainted, taking a angel food cake down with him. He looked better covered in frosting.

Alex came up behind me. He said, "You really should get some business cards printed up. That napkin bit is embarrassing."

We left. I was about to invite Alex back to Do It Right to discuss the day when he said, "I've got to run, Wanda. Tomorrow, crack of dawn."

I said, "See you then." We walked off in opposite directions. I kept my eyes peeled for Martha's lurking strangler. I hailed a cab on Park Avenue and rode home listening to New York's only Caribbean radio station. I felt a bit lonely.

CHAPTER SIX

THE START OF A FESTIVE WEEKEND

On Saturday morning I slept cuddled close to Otis. No kamikaze suicide missions onto my stomach that day. I'd fed her chicken and liver morsels before I crashed. It was 9:30 A.M. Crack of dawn for Alex and me means 10:00. I had to get moving. The phone rang. I said, "Mallory here."

Skip Giddy said, "Morning, angel food."

I said, "Hi, Skip."

"Wanda, I feel terrible."

"What's wrong?"

"You haven't returned my calls."

"I've been busy." I reached over Otis to my nightstand for a cigarette. I torched it and inhaled.

Skip said, "You there?"

I said, "Right here, Skip."

"Look, Wanda. I've got to see you today."

"I'm on deadline." Gladman's word choice.

"Look out the window. The sun is shining, the sky is baby blue. There aren't going to be more days like this left before fall kicks in. You've been busy. I understand that. But I thought a nice day in the country might clear your head. You know, help get a perspective. We can roll around in grassy meadows. Like in wine-cooler commercials. We can talk about us. About your story." I thought of what Alex had said last night at the diner.

I said, "Skip, am I different than the thousands of other women you've fucked?"

He laughed and said, "I wouldn't say thousands."

"Forget it. I can't make it."

"I can get the Beemer out of the garage. We can go north and see the foliage. Breathe fresh air. Wander through a forest." I thought he'd say next, Build a stage in the barn!

I said, "A day in the country, huh?"

"Hot rum and cider."

"Pick me up in an hour."

"Really?" he asked.

I said, "Pick me up in fifty-nine minutes."

Skip made it to the Slope in fifty-seven. Lustable as ever in a red-and-black checkered hunting jacket (shockingly inappropriate for Indian summer), jeans and an oxford. His cheeks were rosy from driving with the windows down, and his hair was tousled in a cute way over his balding spot. He kissed me on the mouth, careening a blaze to my vaginal walls. He told me I looked very downtown—which meant casual. I wore a Gap white T, 501s, and paradise-design Vans. I tied a cashmere cardigan around my waist. He gave me that intense love look that I'm a sucker for. He opened the door for me and then hopped into the driver's seat of his two-door BMW. My hair was loose and wild, and the drive made it worse, or better. We sped toward the Manhattan Bridge, and I told him to turn right onto the Brooklyn-Queens Expressway.

He said, "Where are we going, love cake?"

I said, "Greenwich, Connecticut."

I had gotten Belle's parents' address from information before Skip arrived. Skip drove with bravura, machismo, and any other Italian words that mean "like a raging hard-on." When we hit traffic he pounded the steering wheel and cursed. He let me change gears while he stepped on the clutch. I used to do that with boyfriends in high school. When we hit the wide-open highway he put his hand on my thigh, long fingers worming their way up to my place of origin. I didn't mind. It felt swell, even through jeans.

Nearing Belle's Greenwich home, Skip asked, "Why are we doing this? Haven't these poor people been through enough?"

I said, "It seems the next logical step. Plus she visited them only two weeks ago. She might have said something."

"Why don't you search Belle's apartment in town?"

"Can't. Crime scene. Police seal."

"So can we say that I'm your partner today?"

I replied, "Just do what I tell you. These can be delicate situations."

He leaned over and kissed me. He said, "Wine-cooler commercial later?" I nodded, and we were there.

Skip cranked the emergency brake at the top of the driveway. The house was understated colonial, but worth a bundle. Lots of rolling hills behind it. It was a home that demanded privacy and quiet. Perhaps that's why the Beatrices didn't seem thrilled to see the red BMW tearing up their dirt driveway, blasting James Brown, and sending tiny woodland animals scurrying up trees for safety.

Belle's parents—a proper New England couple—watched us from their rocking chairs on the wood porch, drinking iced tea. I told Skip to stay in the car for a few minutes. I wanted to dip my toe in first. I walked up the steps of the porch and introduced myself. Belle's mother, Anne, said she recognized me from the will reading. Belle's father, Bradley, nodded and sipped his tea. I turned to wave Skip over, but he was halfway up the porch steps already.

"Skip, dear, didn't I ask you to wait in the car?" I said.

He ignored me. "Mr. and Mrs. Beatrice, I want you to know how truly sorry I am about the death of your daughter. She was a great woman, and a dear friend of mine. You may remember me from the funeral. My name is Skip Giddy, an editor at *Shinola* magazine. Not a competitor of *Midnight*'s, but I'm sure if we were, *Midnight* would beat the pants off us. Pleased to meet you." Skip shook hands with Anne and Bradley. They looked at each other and scowled.

Anne was lovely—how Belle would have looked at sixty. Gray hair pulled loosely back, allowing soft wisps to frame her face. She had hazy blue eyes, like a cat with cataracts. Her skin was tightish, only because she was so thin. No face-lift scars.

I said, "Skip is helping me with the investigation." I gave him a warning grin. "At least for today."

Bradley nodded and pursed his lips. He was New

England up and down the gene pool. Square jaw, sharp nose, permanently tan. He was older than Anne, maybe by ten years. He also had blue eyes, but they were sharper and icier than hers. He didn't seem interested in chatting, only in sipping tea and rocking. I directed my questions to Anne. I said, "I thought I'd stop by. See how you're doing. Maybe talk a bit about Belle. That is, if you're up to it."

Anne had a peculiar way of drawling her words. She sounded like Bette Davis on Demerol. She stood and said, "Yes, dear. We'd like to help you. Brad and I liked you when we saw you at the will reading. Didn't we, Father?" Bradley nodded and sipped. She continued, "Of course, Brad and I want the killer found and punished." A gust of Indian summer wind blew through the porch, creaking the chair Anne had just vacated.

I said, "Thank you, Mrs. Beatrice."

Anne said, "Would you like some iced tea? There's more inside."

Skip said, "I sure would, Mrs. Beatrice. The drive dried me right out." Bradley pursed and, the truer mark of disapproval, raised an eyebrow.

Anne asked us to follow her inside. Skip bubbled about peak foliage and fresh air, and Anne patiently smiled. She guided us to the living room through a maze of antique oak and maple furniture. A breeze rustled the lace curtains. While she was in the kitchen I whispered in Skip's ear, "Shut the fuck up, Giddy. I'm running this investigation. Don't you see you're pissing these people off? What the hell is wrong with you?"

He whispered, "I think I can make a positive

contribution here. I've always thought there was a bit of detective in me." Another closet sleuth. Clearly, a simple request wasn't going to work. I offered this instead—the blow job of his life for his deathlike silence during the rest of the visit. He agreed immediately.

Anne came in with a tray of glasses. She eased herself down on the paisley couch and said, "See that urn on the mantel?" We looked. It was porcelain and beautiful in an understated New England way. I nodded. She said, "That's Belle. Brad is very upset about what happened. He doesn't like strangers much either. I don't think we should talk in front of him. Sugar or milk?"

I said, "I'm fine." Skip took both. I sipped and liked the bitterness of the iced tea. I was having trouble swallowing Anne, though. Her decorum tasted artificially sweetened.

"Now, how can I help?" she asked.

I said, "In all honesty, Mrs. Beatrice, I don't know exactly what I'm looking for. Anything you can remember could help. Do you know if Belle had any old enemies, old scores?"

She said, "Belle didn't communicate well with Father and me after she created *Midnight.* Brad hated it, and I—well, I didn't like it much myself. I understand about liberation, including sexual liberation. But we're just from another time, I suppose." She offered Fig Newtons from a plate with apples painted on it. Skip munched a few. Anything to keep his mouth busy, I thought. Anne continued, "We never had actual words with her about the magazine. That's not the way we do things around here. But Father and

I made it clear to Belle that we disapproved." Her slow speech had me on the edge of the couch.

I said, "How'd you do that?"

"Excuse me?" she asked.

"How'd you let Belle know you disapproved of the magazine without telling her?"

Anne's cheeks flushed red. She said, "It wasn't that we didn't let her know, it's that we didn't say anything to her."

So Belle had ESP. "So you and Belle weren't speaking?" I asked.

She shook her head and said, "No. We spoke often. We just didn't speak a certain way with her."

"Belle always spoke lovingly of you," I lied.

Skip said under his breath, "And she gave you all the goodies." She turned to him and pursed. Damn him.

Anne said, "Brad and I were very surprised about that. We've already decided to give most of it away. We'll keep a few personal items, of course. But we are stable financially, and we don't enjoy New York City or the Hamptons. We like our lives here in Greenwich." She sipped her tea and daintily wiped her mouth with a linen napkin.

I said, "Do you know anything about her relationship with Johann Pesto?" I thought he could be a nice segue to any old-lover stories. Particularly someone who like to write erotic poetry.

"Belle never discussed her social life with us," she said.

Belle's friendships were always short and intense. Although I didn't think she'd know, I asked, "Any close friends she mentioned often?"

Anne said, "She never discussed her social life."

"So you didn't talk about the magazine, and you didn't talk about Belle's social life. Forgive me, ma'am, but what did you talk about?"

"Oh, the weather. People in Greenwich. Our talks were more context than content."

"And Belle was satisfied with that?"

Anne said with slow, old-lady indignation, "She never complained. But I will tell you this: There's no question in our minds that the magazine is what got her killed." Another breeze came through, fluttering the curtains.

Skip said, "This fresh air is wonderful." I shot him a warning glance.

"Could you explain that, please?" I asked. "About how the magazine got her killed."

But Anne rolled right over it. "Belle was always a polite, considerate, sweet little girl. A late bloomer. You should have seen her as a teenager. Brad and I thought we'd have to buy her a husband. She was so awkward and thin, with thick glasses. We never imagined she would grow into such a beautiful woman. We were so proud of that." Oh, shit. Like mother, like daughter. Welcome the deluge. Anne used the linen napkin on her eyes. But she didn't let loose the way Belle did. Even in her grief she was the proper Connecticut wife, reserved, dignified, and solid. Only a few salty globules slipped out. Skip motioned to me as if we should do something. I waved him off. She recovered and said with sedate anger, "It wasn't until she started that magazine that she openly confronted Father and me. We didn't know what to do, with the magazine for one thing, and all our friends in town knowing that our daughter was responsible for *that.* Or what to do with Belle's attitude change. Mind you, we loved her as much then as we have our whole lives. It was just the first time we had a serious difference in opinion."

And probably the first time Belle did anything that had to do with love. I didn't think she loved or valued anything more than *Midnight.* I said, "Mrs. Beatrice, what does this have to do with her getting killed?"

She stared at me, her cataract eyes as focused as possible. She said, "Ms. Mallory, don't you see? She had some kind of perverted, demented relationship during her years at that magazine that led to her murder. Think of the kinds of people she met."

People like me. "So you think the killer is someone she met in the last five years?" I asked.

"Or someone she knew before who was horrified by what she'd done." Tiredly she offered Skip more Fig Newtons. He accepted and shoveled them in.

I said, "Do you have any ideas?"

Annoyed, she replied, "Of course I don't." She wriggled a bit, and Skip leapt to her side to help her stand. She smiled at him and said, "Thank you, young man." An appreciator of the old school. I'd have slugged him. She said, "I feel exhausted all of the sudden. Do you mind?"

I stood. I'd struck mud with Anne. And wasted a whole morning. I said, "One more thing, Mrs. Beatrice. Would it be all right if we saw Belle's room?"

She said, "I don't think there's anything up there. Belle hasn't slept here in years. She only came for day trips—and hardly ever at that." She got weepy again.

She took us back outside. We waved good-bye and got in the car.

We were pulling down the driveway—slowly, at my urging. Skip put his hand on my breast and said, "We're alone at last." I removed his hand by the thumb.

"We got squat," I said.

"There are rocks in the quarry, Wanda. They can't all be gems."

I felt a burst of anger. And the pressure of a full bladder.

I said, "Go back."

"Wanda, we're a block away."

"Go back. I've got to take a piss." And get into Belle's bedroom.

He said, "A lawn stop isn't your style?" I glared. He turned the car around.

Anne and Bradley were still on the porch. Mercifully, Skip stayed in the car. I approached them with the universally recognized run-walk. I said quickly, "I'm terribly sorry to disturb you again, but it's a long way back to New York. Do you think I could use the—"

"Follow me." Anne rose again from her chair and led me to the downstairs john.

When I heard Anne leave me I did my business and stealthily split the bathroom without flushing. They'd be listening for that. I climbed the stairs silently, except for when I nearly knocked a bowl of potpourri off a maple table at the top. I passed what looked like the Beatrices' bedroom and a guest bedroom. The only bedroom that could have been Belle's was last on the left. I entered.

I had to shield my eyes from the explosion of gingham and lace. I recovered and moved quickly. Belle must've taken the juicy stuff with her when she moved out. Stuffed lambs and bears crowded the bed. The bookshelves were littered with diaries, paperbacks, and yellowed magazines. There wasn't anything of note in her dresser or desk drawers—only beat-up notebooks with hearts on them and ripped underwear. I couldn't resist peeking at Belle's high school yearbook picture. Anne was right. She was plain as a neighborhood mongrel—brown hair, too, but it wasn't growing up that had made Belle blond. I was about to abandon my search when I remembered to check under the bed. (The stuff I find under *my* bed always solves mysteries.) Sure enough, I spotted one of Belle's favorite day bags. I'd seen her wear it a dozen times; it was the black Hermès leather job she had complained about losing at our lunch at Harry's. I snatched it, ran downstairs, flushed the toilet, and lazily walked onto the porch. I had nowhere to hide the bag. I prayed they wouldn't remember my not walking in with one.

"Thank you again," I said to the Beatrices. The strap on Belle's bag burned a reverse tan line on my shoulder.

Anne looked at it and said slowly, "You're welcome. And good luck."

I got into the car. Skip turned her over, muttering about what is it that women do in bathrooms that takes so goddam long. I noticed Anne and Bradley pointing at us. Suddenly Bradley stood up and strode off the porch toward us. They'd recognized the bag. I resigned myself and got out of the car.

Bradley gripped my shoulder with surprising strength for a man his age. He growled, "Just one minute there."

I held out the bag for him. I said, "I know this seems kooky."

"You find my daughter's killer. You hear me?" He didn't release his grip.

"You don't want the bag?"

"What do I care about your bag? I want you to do your job. Mother and I never got to straighten things out with Belle before she died. Do you understand?"

"Yes, sir," I said. He nodded and released me. We jumped back in the car and drove off. I put Belle's smaller bag into mine. Skip didn't notice, or didn't bother to question me.

He said at the first red light, "God, what a pair of grouches."

I'd felt that kind of frost before when I was at Dartmouth. As Anne said, they have a way of doing things up in New England. Which means being as inviting as an iceberg.

I replied, "It must be something in the water."

When we got onto the highway I told Skip to take me to Do It Right. I wanted to investigate my find. And Alex was probably wondering where I was.

"You used me for my wheels," Skip said.

"Duty calls, babe."

"But I wanted to spend the day with you frolicking in leaf piles and rolling down meadows."

"Some other time."

"What about the piece for *Shinola?* I've discussed it with the bossman, and he loves it. He's counting on me to bring this in."

I said, "I'm working on it."

He said, "Are you? Or should I assign it to someone else? I had to convince him you were the right choice in the first place. And I hate butting heads with the bandleader." Skip turned to me, his green eyes flashing.

The story was my safety net, and my idea. I deserved first crack, and he knew it. I figured Skip was just cranky that I hadn't sucked his dick. I said, "There are a lot of things I want to do for you, Skip." I leaned over the stick shift and kissed him on the neck.

He said, "I'm serious about this, Wanda. Are you going to write the story or not?" I muttered his name in his ear. I've never been much of a name utterer. But men like Skip, the narcissistic types, go chimp shit for it. That's something I didn't have to learn on channel 13. I put my hand inside his hunting jacket. It was nice and sweaty in there. I rubbed his wet oxford and kissed him passionately on the neck. He took one hand off the wheel and put it on the back of my neck, gently massaging my hairline.

I said, "I have a promise to keep." I unbuttoned his jacket and started to unbutton his shirt. I tried to twist my body around the stick shift and accidentally knocked it into neutral. I moved away.

Skip said, "Where're you going, angel? We're OK." He popped the Beemer into fifth. We were doing seventy as I finished unbuttoning his shirt. I sucked on his hairless nipple. His knuckles on the steering wheel were white. His right hand found its way back to my neck, and he was gently nudging my head down. I removed the hand and sucked on his fingers. The car swerved. I put his right hand back on the wheel and told him not to touch me. He rasped affirmative. I pressed the little pup tent of his jeans. Skip lurched. Unzipping his fly was an experiment in delicacy. One pothole and we'd be racing to the nearest emergency room. I reached for the knob on the Benzi box and cranked up the volume. The sounds of a blow job can be such a turnoff—all that slurping and smacking. Instead, the primal gruntings of James Brown engulfed the little Beemer as we rambled down the road to sexual oblivion.

Once unzipped, Skip's dick bobbed and swayed to the rhythm of the asphalt. I studied it for a while. It was a nice prick. Bent the right way, conservative length, daring width. Skip looked down at me curled sideways around the stick shift, leaning on his legs. His expression was reminiscent of Johann's at the Orchid Lounge. I smiled, told him to keep his eyes on the road, and dug in. I don't think he heard any unpleasant spit sloshings, what with the funk master yelping for mercy and all.

I finished him off right before the Triboro Bridge. I sat up and pushed in the cigarette lighter on the dash. The driver in the Mitzvah Winnebago in the next lane doffed his yarmulke to me. Skip had done a fine job of keeping us alive. I said, "Sure, I'll do the story. But you've just got to wait."

He said, "I can wait."

"Good. Now take me to Do It Right."

Skip pulled up in front of my office on 42nd Street. There was a vaguely familiar man in sunglasses, a floppy hat, and a trench coat leaning against the deli storefront window on the bottom floor of my building. I gave Skip a kiss good-bye. When I turned back around the man was gone. I walked up to four.

Alex was behind my desk. He said, "Where the hell have you been? I've been waiting here for hours. And who the hell owns that red BMW?" The office was spotless; he must have been worried.

"How did you know I was in a red BMW?" I asked.

"Santina saw you leave this morning," he replied.

"I want to show you something."

"Yeah, yeah, I want to show you something, too, but first tell me where you've been, and why it was physically impossible to call." He crossed his arms over his thin chest, and his hair fell into his eyes. He raked it back with a paw. He said, "I'm waiting."

I pulled Belle's purse out of mine and tossed it on my desk. The weight made the short leg wobble. "Exhibit A: Belle's missing luggage, which I cleverly whisked out of her parents' house in Greenwich this morning."

Alex said, "No shit. Great. I didn't mean to imply that you weren't working. I assumed you were working, but still." Alex picked up Belle's bag and put it to his nose. He inhaled and said, "It's leather all right."

"Sorry I didn't call. I was distracted."

"So then you *were* with Skip."

"Let's not go through this again."

"He's such an asshole," Alex said.

"Stop." I sat down on the phone book in my chair. Belle's bag didn't have much in it; just an almost-new lipstick, siren red, and two letters. We each took one.

Alex's was on white Eaton typing paper. It read:

Ode to Belle's Nipples

They seem to stare, my beloved's nipples,
Directing their gaze at my eager member, teasing,
Testing. Raisins slipped into her blouse,
Fully withered by the heat they contain,
Yet inflated and plump,
Begging the cool breath of my lips.

Alex said, "I'm ashamed to admit it, but some of these poems are getting me hot."

I said, "Listen to this. It's a note from Herb to Belle. Dated Friday, October fifth. It says, 'Dear Belle—Your proposition is an intriguing one. I want two weeks to consider it. *Midnight* means more to me than you think. I'm sure we can work things out. I've had harder jobs than loving you. See you Monday. Herb.'"

Alex said, "I didn't know they were having an affair."

"That's exactly what Skip said at the funeral. We may be jumping to conclusions. Herb said he didn't write that poem."

"But wouldn't you lie to protect yourself?"

"I guess we should put Herb back on the suspect list." I picked up the phone to give him a call.

"No, don't warn him. Let's go after him quietly," Alex said. I put down the phone.

"So what were Belle's parents like?" Alex asked.

"Like a blizzard at Mardi Gras."

"No fun?"

"A bit chilly." I flashed to the picture of nerd Belle in high school. She had never told me about that time in her life. I wondered what other secrets she'd kept. I missed her.

Alex and I dined with Santina that night. We'd spent the afternoon doing nothing productive. We tried to make some connections between exploding come balloons, murder, and bad poetry but saw nothing but general kinkiness. And there were still some questions about the alleged attack on Martha. We called Gladman, and he confirmed that they'd worked late Thursday night. Although Alex told me to relax, I was worried that someone at Stephanopoulos's would report me to the cops. So I shouldn't have pulled Mama on Cosmos. So I can be impatient. But if he hadn't talked to the police yet, he might never.

Santina distracted us pretty well. I agreed to eat with her only if she promised not to mention the following subjects: law school, Times Square, my sex life, and the case. She crossed her heart and swore on her secret mixture of tint #34 and dye #47 ("a shimmering gold/auburn—makes men swoon") not to. She leaned over the stove and cracked raw eggs into hot pasta to make fettuccini carbonara. Alex and I sat at the table, dipping chunks of baguette into vinaigrette. Santina's two-floor apartment is designed to satisfy her two basic needs—the kitchen and dining room on one floor, the bedroom upstairs. Knickknacks, souvenirs, and pictures clutter every flat surface. She's a collector, and not one to hide secrets.

Santina furiously stirred the eggs in and said, "You! Both of you. Get away from that. That's for the salad later." She threatened us with a wooden spoon. "And Alex, put your napkin in your lap, for chrissake. What do you think this is? A barn?" Alex did as he was told, but not without making a face.

I said, "Santi, relax. You'll frighten him." I smiled at Alex.

Santi said, "Frighten, shmighten. Alex and I have scrubbed toilets together. Haven't we, honey? And get your napkin in your lap, Ms. I Have Better Manners Than You. So, back to my story. I said to him, I said, 'Fine, Shlomo. Go ahead. Drown for all I care.' "

I said, "It sounds fun, Santi."

"Fun to you, Ms. Adventureland. I can't see a single nice thing in Shlomo taking the Mercedes and leaving me alone in Brooklyn while he goes sailing off Rhode Island with that desperado from the Learning Annex."

Alex said, "The prosciutto and melon are great, Santina."

"The melon isn't ripe. I shook every single one at the Korean deli today. And believe you me, I gave them a piece of my mind. So kill me. I serve you unripe melon."

"Whose yacht is it anyway?" I asked.

Santi said, "The fake blonde who teaches the sailing class. Hideous frosted eyeshadow and opalescent lip gloss. Enough to make you want to toss in your blushing pad. She gets her hair done at Georgette Klinger. Spare me. The pathetic thing has absolutely no taste." Santi dug the spoon into the pot and sampled the pasta. "Eh. It'll do. Come on, bring your plates over here." She motioned us over with the spoon. She continued, "So he says to me, he says, 'Santina, I'll only be gone two days.' So I said to him, 'Long enough for me to have a nervous breakdown.' "

"How many other students went?" Alex asked. I stuck my hand into the pot and snagged a prime sliver of bacon. Santina smacked the back of my hand with the spoon.

She said to me, "Can't you wait?" She dished out a mountain to Alex and an anthill to me. She shook her head and blew out her cheeks when I asked for more. She said to Alex, "I don't know how many other students went. But I'm telling you, if I ever find out that number is none, Shlomo can just pack his bags and move back to his hoity-toity Upper East Side for all I care. Let that bimbo sleep with him. Like I care? Like I give two shits? Like this is affecting me in any way, shape, or form?" Alex and I didn't have to be detectives to see that it was. But I knew Shlomo. A man who takes courses at the Learning Annex seriously, a closet horticulturist who has orgasms at the mention of juniper, a doctor who moved to Brooklyn to humor a loony beautician with a thing for "colorful surroundings"—could this man be deceptive? But Santi knows him better than I. And she likes to maintain a healthy tension in their relationship. It helps reaffirm her irrational fear of marriage.

We ate. Santina barely sat still. Trips for salt, pepper, wine, parmesan. Finally Alex said, "Santina. You know—"

"What? More bread? More wine? You want more already, sweetheart? You young men can sure pack it away."

"I just wanted to offer a bit of advice," Alex said.

"Fire away. I love hearing the thoughts of the younger generation. Please, you've got both ears. Go right ahead."

He said, "Okay. I'd say there's one thing men want from their women, more than any other thing."

I said, "Sex."

He said, "Well, sure, but that's not what I meant. Men want their women to trust them. More than anything else."

That shut both of us up. And stopped us eating. Alex shoveled it in and didn't seem to notice that we'd put our forks down. I listened to the fridge hum.

Santina spoke first. She said, "Well, Alex. Catch me looking like an old fool, why don't you?" She paused. "Are you sure you don't want more?"

He held up his empty plate and said, "I'd love some more. Thanks."

Santina gave Alex one of her rare non-tainted smiles. She took his plate and walked to the kitchen. I got up and followed her with my empty plate. Her perfectly made-up face had fallen, a strange contradiction to her high-piled hair.

In the kitchen I said, "He's right, you know."

Uncharacteristically soft-spoken, Santina said, "Maybe I should marry Shlomo."

"Maybe you should." Alex walked in and reached into the fridge for the salad. He told Santi that he'd forgotten about the greens and, even though the pasta was ambrosial, he'd just as soon pass on seconds and save some room for dessert. All this talk of food snapped Santi back to her usual enthusiasm. She snatched the salad from Alex and began dishing it into small bowls. She buoyantly described her day-long odyssey searching for this dazzling array of vegetables and gossiped about the cashiers at all the epicurean shops in Park Slope. I stepped behind her and tried to spoon out another helping of pasta for myself. Santi took my plate away and dumped the remaining pasta in the garbage.

"I think you've had enough, Ms. I Don't Have to Diet."

I shrugged. No one but Santina seemed to mind how much I ate. I walked over to the dining room and lit a cigarette.

"So how is the investigation going?" Santina asked.

Alex replied, "Okay. Lots of bizarre clues with no solid leads."

"Bizarre how?"

"Attacks on the street, erotic poetry, come balloons."

I said, "Alex, don't talk about the case in front of her."

Santina assured us we could, but I knew better. We'd just begun to eat the salad when she started up.

"Oh, before I forget to mention," she said, "I've got law school applications in the other room. I think it would do you good just to fill them out. All of them. This goes for you, too, Alex. We can go through them tonight after coffee. Ginger tea for Wanda, of course. I know I promised to shut up, but really, Ms. Private Eye, you're in danger. I can feel it. There's trouble in that disgusting Times Square office. I know you still take that shortcut through the construction to get there, too. Trouble. I can't take this anymore. When Shlomo gets home you'll get a word from him, too."

So I'd have that to look forward to. After dessert—

Alex got peach melba, I got half a grapefruit—we slipped down to my apartment.

It was ten o'clock. We sat on my couch, stuffed from the wonderful meal. Otis lay between us, purring loudly. Alex rubbed her between the ears. I said, "Tomorrow we should go after Herb and get the truth about their alleged secret affair. And we should reread those poems. Maybe we overlooked something."

"Do you really think he had anything to do with the attack?" Alex asked.

"I'm still having trouble believing that attack ever happened. But they say Herb matches the body type. I've never seen him wear a hat, though." I remembered the man I spotted outside Do It Right with the floppy hat.

"All things make themselves evident," Alex said. "We just have to wait."

Otis stretched each leg separately and jumped down. She trotted to the bowl I'd given her; prime grill for dinner. I said, "Alex, I liked what you said up there."

"What?"

"What you said to Santina about Shlomo. About trust."

"Oh, that."

"I liked it a lot." It turned me on, in fact. That and the wine.

He said, "Good."

"Did you mean it?"

"Yeah."

"So trust is that important?"

"It is for me."

I looked at the clock on the VCR. I said, "You can

stay here tonight if you don't want to go back to your apartment." Alex lives in a nondescript one-bedroom on Delancey Street. It stays noisy until pretty late.

He said, "Okay. Thanks."

"Unless you have to be somewhere else." I meant the girlfriend's.

"Where would I have to be?"

"I don't know. The darkroom." His euphemism.

He said, "I'm taking the night off." I did the analytical girl thing. Does that mean he's taking the night off from his woman to have some sex-between-friends action with me, or is it that they had a fight and he can't deal with her right now, or that he's taking the night off from women altogether by being with his colleague, me? I decided to try anyway. I inched over to him, closing the gap Otis had created. I said, "Do you trust me?"

He looked at me, shielding his eyes by squinting. He said, "You're not my woman."

I put my hand on his knee and said, "I trust you." I kissed him on the cheek. He closed his eyes. I toyed with his ear. I kissed him again. He shifted on the sofa and gently pushed me away.

He said, "No, Wanda."

"What do you mean, no?"

"It's quite simple, really."

"So you're saying no?"

"Yes, I'm saying no."

I said, "What the hell do you mean by that?"

"You've got a boyfriend, remember?" It took me a full minute to realize he was talking about Skip.

"He doesn't have anything to do with you." But by that time my daring urge had passed.

He didn't look at me when he replied, "It's late, Wanda. Why don't we go to sleep?" The tone was far from bantering.

"I'll get you a blanket," I said. "For the couch."

"The couch is fine."

I found an extra blanket and caseless pillow in my room. The physical distance from him helped. What had I been thinking? I threw the stuff at him when I returned. I said, "Here. I hope you choke on them."

"Thanks." He smiled to himself.

"What mirth, Mr. Hilarity?"

"You're so tough. But you act like a spoiled brat when you don't get what you want."

"Like you have any idea what I want?"

"I think I'm learning."

Otis cantered down the hall after me to my bedroom. I performed my nocturnal ablutions and got into bed. I made a mental note to explore my trust history. And I made an observation: Playing hard-to-get works.

CHAPTER SEVEN

A BOUNTY OF SURPRISE

Alex didn't wake me when he split Sunday morning. He left a note on my kitchen table that said to meet him at Do It Right at noon. Only three days left in the investigation. It was yet another beautiful day. I caught the D train and took my shortcut through the construction. I was twenty minutes early. I thought I saw the familiar man in the floppy hat from half a block away, but he wasn't around when I got to the building. The light was blinking on the answering machine. First there were some suggestive breathing noises. Then he said, "I'm waiting for you." It sounded like he'd tried to disguise his voice. I didn't recognize it. I felt a chill. I hoped Alex would hurry up. I toyed with makeup from the first-aid kit to kill time. I should have remembered to buy coverup for prison pallors like mine—all I've got is the tan stuff ("for Puerto Rican girls," according to Santina).

When Alex finally arrived I played the message for him. He thought it was just a random obscene caller. I wasn't so sure. We took the F train to West 4th Street to stake out Herb's studio on Waverly Place in the West Village. To further brighten my day, the train's air conditioning was busted. Throngs of New Jersey and Long Island weekend tourists clogged Sixth Avenue, along with the countless street vendors selling bad incense, worse jewelry, and exceptional (in their own way) velvet celebrity portraits. Kids played one-hoop ball on the asphalt court across from the kiosk pinwheel. We bought a few bagels and coffee (tea for me) and sat on a convenient stoop across the street from Herb's building. We waited. It was around 12:30. I knew for a fact that Herb reads the *Times* cover to cover every Sunday morning and never leaves his apartment before 1:00 P.M. He bragged of this often at *Midnight*. We ate our breakfasts.

Neither of us mentioned the previous night's kiss. I was thinking about it, though. I hoped it wouldn't cause any problems in the investigation.

I thought about the possibility that Herb and Belle were lovers. Herb reveled in Belle's attention—just like everyone else at *Midnight*. That so much of it was flirtatious never seemed to bother him. In fact, Herb used to brag about it. A secret affair wasn't totally out of the question. Alex suggested that, because we found the nipple poem in her purse along with Belle's letter, Herb could very well be the poet, and possibly the killer. I wasn't sure how Alex and I would handle him that Sunday. Herb was a friend of mine. I didn't want to accuse him of anything. If he spotted us, we'd have to improvise. If not, we'd just get to know Herb's private life a little better.

Like clockwork, Herb emerged into the Indian

summer afternoon at 1:00. We hid behind newspapers as he walked by us on the other side of the street. He was dressed up, in a gray lightweight Valentino suit with a white laundromat hanky in the breast pocket. (I wore my glasses that day and could see all.) Alex and I slowly descended our stoop and came up a few yards behind Herb as he rounded the corner on Sixth Avenue. I was wearing all black for covert surveillance —possibly a bad choice. The sun was roasting me. Alex was par normal in 501s.

Herb stopped in a liquor store. He bought a pint of blackberry brandy. "Gross," I whispered to Alex. He didn't comment. Next stop, the post office. Herb pulled a letter from his pocket, used the stamp machine, and dropped it in the out-of-state box. "I wish we could've seen who that was addressed to," Alex muttered to me. Another stop was at the Store 24 on Greenwich Avenue. Herb withdrew some cash—quite a bit, in fact—from the quick-stop cash machine inside. He bought a bag of Pepperidge Farm goldfish, parmesan. Once outside he put the money in with the fish. Things were beginning to get interesting.

The next stop was at a swanky downtown eatery called Knickerbockers. The front is a big window, which made things nice for Alex and me. But the darkness inside, especially because of the brightness outside, made it hard to see. We watched from the street; Herb's back was to us. He sat in a red upholstered booth and ordered a drink. In a few minutes a man joined Herb. I recognized him from the funeral; he was Max Rudberg, CEO and president of Foxboro Corporation. The magazine stock was held by the Foxboro Corporation, as well as Belle's private portfolio. I didn't remember seeing Rudberg talk to Herb at the funeral. The one thing I knew they had in common was that Belle could never seduce either.

They laughed and talked as they ate a late lunch. When Herb gave Rudberg the blackberry brandy and the bag of goldfish I felt sure we were on to something. Maybe Rudberg, as he liquidated Belle's stocks, thought he could slide himself some booty for the effort—a cut of Beatrice Publishing, perhaps? All that stock was under Herb's care. Maybe they knew about the will and had planned to kill Belle so they could arrange her stocks to pad their respective nests. But what of the money in the goldfish? It was at least a few hundred. That might not be much to a man like Rudberg, but to a man like Herb it was a lot. A bribe? A payoff? Did Rudberg catch Herb screwing around with the stock and blackmail him? There were so many options. All of which added up to no good.

They finished lunch and parted with a manly handshake. After they left, Alex and I decided to ask the waitress if she'd overheard anything. We found her by the bar. I hadn't gotten a good enough look at her from the street, all my attention having been on Herb and Rudberg. When we got close, I didn't like what I saw.

You could easily imagine the healthy red corpuscles swimming through her virgin arteries. She was peaches-and-cream to a fault. And cute. Who isn't at seventeen? She blinked innocent blue eyes and lazily tossed a glorious mane of blond hair over her birdbone shoulders. Alex stretched to his full six feet, leaned cock-forward, and grinned madly at her.

"How many?" she asked.

I said, "We don't want food. We want information."

She was taken aback. Alex took over. He said, "Excuse her. We were just wondering about the two gentlemen who were sitting over there." He pointed to the empty booth.

She ran a manicured fingernail over her plump lips. She said, "You just missed them. They left."

Alex said, "I know. We watched them go. I think I recognized one of them as an old family friend. You didn't happen to overhear any of their conversation?"

She giggled and flashed her teeth. "What's going on here? Are you a cop or something?" It immediately occurred to me that unless she had overheard something suspicious, she wouldn't assume we were police. She kept on smiling at Alex. I didn't like it.

I said, "Do we look like cops?"

She replied, "I guess not, but you never know anymore. A city gal has to be careful these days." Belle had to learn that the hard way. Alex was staring at the waitress and rubbing his stomach unconsciously.

"Do you model?" he asked the jailbait.

She squirmed on her bar chair and purred, "No, but I've been looking into it."

He said, "I used to shoot for fashion magazines. You could easily get work. Your cheekbones are spectacular."

I couldn't believe what I was hearing.

She said, "They are?"

"What's your name?" Alex asked flirtatiously.

"Candie."

Alex smiled, showing his teeth. He never does that, even when he flirts. "Candie," he said, "the truth is that the man isn't an old family friend." He put his hand on the back of her chair. His wrist brushed her bare shoulder. She leaned into it like a cat and stared up at him. I made a mental note to go on a diet.

She said, "Who is he, then?"

Alex said, "He's my father. I haven't seen him in ten years. We . . . we had a falling out. I'm not even sure that was him. Did he use a name, say anything you remember?"

She batted her lashes and said, "That's so sad. I bet you miss him."

He said, "I miss him bad." Alex looked at his feet and hid his eyes. Candie actually stood up and hugged him. I couldn't help noticing that her breasts didn't give with the press. He put his arms around her and hugged back. My female omniscience told me he was flirting for real. And he talks about trust! I even fantasized about squealing to his girlfriend. He continued, "Any snippet of conversation would help."

She said, "Give me a second to think. Here, have my seat." He sat down, and she kept a hand on his shoulder. What a lovely couple.

I sat down in one of the chairs to watch this nauseating scene. I whipped out a cigarette from my bag, lit it, and patted Mama.

Candie breathed, "Wait. They did say something, I remember." Alex looked up with cow eyes. I leaned over. Candie turned to me and scowled. I waved at her. She turned back to Alex and asked, "Who is she?"

He stage-whispered, "My sister. You see, I've squandered my inheritance on my art. I'm a painter. And my sister won't give me a cent of the family trust unless we find Father and get his approval." Sympathy seeped from her face.

Candie gnawed on a swizzle stick and whispered back, "I hate her for that."

Their eyes latched. I've seen that look before; it usually ends with four bare legs in a bed. He'd skyrocketed past the requirements of a flirt scam. I'd seen enough.

I stood and said, "Look, this kid isn't going to help you. Let's go." I grabbed Alex by the wrist. "I said we're leaving now."

Alex didn't budge. With more vehemence than necessary I said, "Who's in charge here, Alex?"

Candie, perceptive little pixie, said, "Cool out, lady." She turned to him and said, "They got real quiet whenever I came over, but I do remember hearing them talk about a meeting planned for later tonight. The younger one said he hoped everyone would show up, especially some banker or something." So they were planning a secret meeting with another banker. Signing over some of the Beatrice estate, no doubt. I couldn't believe I was finding these things out about Herb. Just goes to show you—don't trust anyone. Before we left, Candie gave Alex her phone number on a cocktail napkin. Tacky. She made some teenage vixen noises about seeing Alex real soon, and he promised he'd call.

Once outside, Alex gave me a dirty look. I said, "Maybe you'd like to kiss *her*."

He said, "Don't start with me, Mallory. You almost blew it."

"Blew what—your shot as a statutory rapist?"

"If it wasn't for me, we'd be standing in there holding our dicks."

"I don't have a dick," I said.

He said, "Excuse me. Sometimes I forget." I let him have the last bark. I'll swallow anything once, including my rapierlike wit.

The sun was still high, and there were more people milling around the Village. A tarot-card reader with a bridge table gestured enticingly at the passersby. Two men kissed on the hood of an Impala. After the moment of tension passed, we agreed to confront Herb. On the walk back to West 4th Street Alex was unusually quiet. He didn't make eye contact with me. I'm not hard to look at, but I didn't come close to Candie in the glamour-nymph department. I wished I hadn't yelled at him. I checked my watch; it was just before 4:00.

I'd never been inside Herb's apartment before. There was no doorman at his standard Village brownstone. Another tenant left as we approached, so we didn't have to buzz to be let in. We saw from the list by the bell that Herb lived on the first floor. We knocked at his door.

A stunningly attractive man with a long tan body answered. He was wearing purple Calvin Klein briefs and a green bandanna wrapped around his head. We identified ourselves as Herb's friends. He asked us to come in.

I said, "Nice Frisbee helmet."

He said, "Do you like it? It's a new look for me."

I said, "It works. You have the right shape of head." He was completely comfortable in his underwear; a man after my own heart.

"I just got a new haircut. I don't love it at all." He

took off the bandanna and showed us. I didn't think it looked so bad—with a face like that, you couldn't go wrong.

I said, "I wouldn't worry about it."

"I got it for an audition; I'm an actor. I didn't get the part, of course. And now I'm stuck looking like G.I. Joe. Wait right here, I'll get Herb." And he left us to examine the surroundings. An ad in the *Times* would describe it as "a sunny one-bedroom with wood floors and high ceilings." The walls in the common room were painted pink. Nice, modest decor. If I were to design my own apartment, I'd do it like Herb's. Shelving covered the wall with no windows. On the shelving was a jungle of plants, mainly philodendron types, a few spiders and ferns. The furniture was all wood, tastefully and conservatively designed. Track lighting on the ceiling. Alex commented on a framed poster of a photograph I knew I'd seen before, but I didn't know where. Two men's heads in profile.

"Mapplethorpe," Alex told me.

Herb the bear came in wearing Valentino. "Wanda, Alex, what a surprise," he said slowly.

I said, "A pleasant one, I hope."

He said, "You met Larry."

I said, "He's lovely."

"Yes, he is. We share the apartment." Herb grinned.

I just got it.

I said, "So how come you never told me?"

He said dourly, "I didn't think it was important to our professional relationship."

"But we have a friendship, too."

"If we had a friendship, wouldn't you know that I'm gay?"

I let that sink in.

"I assume Belle didn't know either."

"Sure she knew. Belle and I were close."

"So how come she always came on to you?"

"It was part of our friendship. We enjoyed flirting, and it was safe because we knew nothing would ever happen." Like me and Alex. I looked over at him, and he purposely avoided eye contact. Still mad, I figured.

"So what about this letter?" I asked, and I gave him the note.

He glanced at it and said, "What about it? I got a job offer at another magazine, and the idea of a change looked pretty good to me. Belle offered me more money, but no title change. I wanted some time to consider. That's all the note says. What did you think—that we were having a secret affair?"

I said, "What about the 'loving you isn't the hardest job I ever had' part?"

He said, "Didn't you love her, too?"

I suddenly felt like more of an idiot than usual. "We've been following you," I said.

Herb threw his head back and laughed. He said, "So I'm a bad guy now? I love it." He called into the other room: "Larry! I'm a bad guy."

I said, "We watched you put mucho dinero in the goldfish and give it to Rudberg. What gives?"

"That had nothing to do with Belle's death."

"But what about Belle's money?" Alex asked.

Larry came out of the bedroom looking spectacular in a maroon Armani suit. He put a hand on Herb's shoulder and said, "Of course you're a bad guy. Are you ready? Max is probably waiting at the club."

Herb covered Larry's hand and said, "One minute." He turned to us. "We're going to an ACT-UP party at my men's club on Cornelia Street. Max Rudberg is a member. The bag of goldfish is the door prize. It's a joke. The winner gets it, thinks he's been gypped. Then he opens it up and sees the bills. And it's hardly mucho dinero, Wanda. It's only fifty bucks."

Larry said, "It's a stupid idea. I don't love it at all."

Herb nodded in agreement. "Max's idea," he said. "I'd appreciate it if you could keep him out of this. He's still protective of his sexuality. A lot of the club members are. If you want to come along as my guests, you're invited. It's for a good cause."

"Another time," I said. We thanked Herb and left. I planned to check on all this, but Herb's story did explain why Belle never got him and Max in the sack. I lit a cigarette when we got outside. It tasted swell.

When Alex and I returned to Do It Right that afternoon the first thing I did was check for more obscene calls. There were none. Alex dropped his wallet and keys on my desk before he went down to the hall to the bathroom. On a search-and-destroy mission I went through Alex's wallet and found the cocktail napkin with Candie's phone number on it. I ripped it up and ate it. Just saving him from jailbait. He'd thank me later.

When he came back I handed him half the pile of love poems we'd accumulated. We were looking for anything—a recurring theme, a busted typewriter key—anything. I lit a cigarette. I'd been smoking a lot lately. Alex coughed. He said, "Can you please blow that out the window?" Candie probably didn't smoke. Candie probably didn't cut her own meat.

I said, "No problem," but I forgot after a few puffs. With a harumph Alex took his pile and moved his chair across the room.

He saw me watching. He said, "What's your problem?"

"No problem," I said.

I focused on the poems and wondered if Belle had been turned on by them. I remembered Belle telling me once, "The only things that excite me anymore are multiple orgasms and magazine awards." I looked at Alex. He hadn't spoken much since we'd left Herb's.

I said, "I can't believe Herb was thinking about leaving *Midnight*. Belle must have had a fit."

Alex didn't look up. He said, "Change is good. Look how your life changed when you left." I wondered if Alex was thinking of leaving Do It Right. He didn't seem too happy with me.

"What are you trying to tell me?" I asked.

"Change is good, that's all."

"You're making an obvious comparison between Herb and Belle and me and you." The analytical girl thing was taking over again.

"What are you talking about?"

I said, "He was thinking of leaving her, like you're thinking of leaving me."

"I'm not thinking about that at all," he said. "Do you want me to leave the agency?"

"If you want to go, then go."

He looked hard at me. I think I hurt him. He said, "I asked if you want me to go."

I said, "You don't seem very happy. Maybe you'd be happier someplace else." He stood up and paced the room. "No, I mean I don't want you to leave," I blurted out.

"I don't want to leave either," he said quietly. We made the first eye contact of the day. So that was taken care of. I wondered why I still felt tense.

Alex suggested we order in some food. I picked up the phone and dialed the deli downstairs to get some sammies. Alex volunteered to go get them. He checked his money situation while I was on the phone.

The voice said, "Deli Express." Alex inspected his wallet with a look of angry realization. He took two giant steps toward me and banged his knuckles on my desk. I could tell by his expression that it'd be a while before I saw any food. I said into the phone, "Just a second."

Alex said, "Hang up."

I covered the mouthpiece with my hand and said, "What did you say you wanted again? Tuna on rye?"

The deli man said into my ear, "Lady, I don't got all day."

Alex said, "Hang up."

With an attempt at humor, I said, "What's the magic word?"

"Now," he said.

The deli man said, "You want to order or what?"

Alex wrenched the receiver from my hand and slammed it down. I said, "You seem upset."

"You're damned right I'm upset. Where's Candie's phone number?"

"You must have lost it." So I lied to protect myself.

"I think you lost it for me."

"What do I care about that prepubescent minx?"

"Just tell me where it is, and we'll forget the whole thing."

"I don't have it."

Anger colored his ears red, but Alex gulped down whatever vexation clogged his throat. He said, "Well, it doesn't matter. I can go see her if I want. But I think we should make some things clear, Wanda. If you do want me to stay at Do It Right, don't get involved in my personal affairs."

I said, "Don't you find it interesting that you can say just about anything to me about Skip, and if I show any mild—and I mean mild—interest in your affairs, you spin gaskets."

"You want to do this?" he asked. "Okay. Let's talk personality flaws." Alex used his fingers to count them off. "You're selfish, self-absorbed, controlling, and crass. You think you're the only one who knows anything about detecting or talking to a witness. You're insensitive. And then there's the other issue."

"What other issue?" I asked.

"You don't have any idea what romance is about," he said.

"If that were true, I don't see what that has to do with you anyway."

"You had your tongue halfway down my ear last night, remember?"

"Are you referring to my platonic little kiss? My harmless gesture of friendly affection?"

That got him. He walked toward the door. He focused on the coatrack and said, "Ever since that so-called platonic kiss last night you've been jerking me around, treating me like a ten-year-old, and lying to me. And I don't like it. It's obvious that you aren't so sure what you want from me. You aren't even sure if you want me to work here. So when you figure all this out, you give me a call." He paused, then said solemnly, "I don't give a shit about Candie. And I'm surprised you thought I did. Really, give me a little more credit." Alex gently pulled the door shut behind him. I got up and slammed it properly.

Around ten that night I decided to take a turn around Times Square. Alex had been gone for hours. Right before my walk the phone rang. I hoped it was Alex. It was the obscene caller. He said, with the muffled voice, "I'm watching you," and hung up. I felt cold and claustrophobic. I called Alex on Delancey Street, but he didn't pick up. I locked the office door and jogged down the four flights; it's not a good idea to take the elevator late at night. I walked quickly up Broadway, moving with the rhythm of the street. As I passed a shoe store I glanced at my reflection in the window. For a moment I thought I saw the man in the floppy hat behind me. I kept going. As I passed the next storefront, I peeked in the window to see if he was still there. He wasn't. I stopped and pretended to play with my hair. No one approached me. I shook my head out and rubbed my eyes. I must be hallucinating, I thought. I felt a tap on my shoulder. I spun around, one hand in my bag, ready to pull out Mama. It was a Salvation Army officer. He asked me if I was okay. I told him to fuck off and kept walking, looking for a place to go.

The bouncers had the night off at the Orchid Lounge. I ducked in. Might as well ask a few questions about Johann and Martha. It was a slow night at the Orchid. I'd already gulped a few shots of Amaretto at the office, nearly depleting the client liquor supply. Luigi mixed a margarita on the rocks with salt. No harm in treating myself to a little mescal on a lonely Sunday night. Luigi leered his toothless chasm when I took my first slug. He said he remembered me from the night with Martha and Johann. He kept calling me Hand-Job.

The jalapeño bulbs on the ceiling blinked, and I wondered what the bottomless cocktail waitresses did when they had their periods. I asked Luigi, interrupting his story about three Okie stewardesses from Muskogee. He chortled and continued his epic. I let it pass. The margarita seeped down my throat like mink oil on leather. I flashed back to the old days in New Jersey when I soaked my Rawlings third-baseman's mitt in Mazola. I kept my eye on the door for the man in the floppy hat. I continued poisoning my gut with tequila.

Luigi scrubbed the bar top with a rusty rag. I must have been swaying. He asked if I was okay. I couldn't take concern from a toothless porn impresario seriously, so I told him to get lost. He did, but he came back with a friend. He said, "Hey, Hand-Job. Why don't you suckle on this little darling for a while?" I hazily glanced up. Next to Luigi stood one of the bottomless waitresses.

She said, "You look depressed."

"What do you do when you have your period?" I asked.

Luigi said, "This is Deb. She makes friends easy."

She had ruby-red lips, gold-sparkled eyelids, brown pony-tails sticking out pugnaciously over each ear, a heart-shaped face, and an incredible body.

I said, "I don't fuck women."

Deb said, "You look like you need someone to talk to."

I pointed at my drink. "That's all the help I need."

Deb jerked some dirty glasses over an oversized fish-tank brush. She said, "Luigi says he's a friend of yours."

"I don't have any friends."

"I'll be your friend."

I said, "I didn't say I wanted any."

"I'm not trying to pick you up."

"I didn't say you were." I took another slug; oil on leather.

"I'm just trying to talk to you."

"I don't want company. You can't swing a dead cat in here without hitting someone who does. Go talk to those guys if you're looking for conversation." I pointed at some men chatting with Luigi.

She said, "Luigi is taking care of them." She put a bottle of mescal on the bar. "Talking to you is like opening a can with a fork." That sounded like something I would say. She twisted a ponytail. I focused my tequila goggles on her. I'd guess she was in her early twenties. Her eyes offered more than an inkling of intelligence. Just another lonely Sunday night for her, too, I guessed. Suddenly I figured it couldn't hurt to share my wealth of misery with this lonely Orchid urchin. "So, Deb. What do you want to talk about?" I asked.

She said, "Let's talk about you."

I'd rather be gang-raped by sweaty lumberjacks, I thought. I said, "I don't like to talk about myself."

"Why not?"

"My problems are my business."

"Other people can help you with your problems."

I said, "It's crowded enough in here." I tapped my cranium with the edge of my glass. The ice clinked. I needed another drink. Deb poured one for me.

"On the house," she said.

"Thanks." I kicked back the concoction in one swallow. She splashed me another.

"What do you do for a living?" she asked.

"What do *you* do for a living? Oh—scratch that. I already know."

"You only know half. I'm a grad student. I'm one year into the master's program at NYU in clinical psychology. And actually I have a little confession to make. I'm testing my homework on you."

"You're not doing too well," I said.

"Not yet." She fidgeted with a strap of her bikini top and twirled a ponytail.

"Okay. So what's the assignment?" I asked.

"It's not a real assignment," she said. "I just like to talk to people who look like they need a friend. A little free-lance work."

"You and Luigi—tag-team do-gooders."

"You can tease me if you want. But I like to help out."

"I bet sucking off Neanderthals for a ten-spot is part of your mission?"

"Head costs fifty," she said, smiling.

Well, blow me down. This obviously wasn't your average grad student. Or your average backroom humper. I said, "If you want to help me, tell me if you've even balled a tall blond named Johann Pesto."

"Sure, I know Johann. He used to come in a lot with presents for the girls." The handcuffs and penis-handled feather duster I saw him buy at the Snack Happy, no doubt. She continued, "He hasn't been around so much lately now that he's a celebrity. I think he's got a regular date."

"You must mean Martha Schpreckenspiel. Tall, long brown hair."

"I've never seen him with her," she said. "He just told me one night that he was getting married." He must have meant Belle.

"When was that?"

"A week ago."

"Did he ever talk about a woman named Belle Beatrice?"

Deb smiled and said, "She was my hero, you know."

"Mine, too," I said.

She wiped the bar down with the dirty rag. She poured mescal into her shot glasses. She said, "Can I buy you another shot?"

I said, "Hit me." She downed hers. I reached for my glass and knocked it over, sending mescal dribbling down the bar. I was drunker than I thought.

Deb said, "Boy trouble?"

"I don't want to talk about it."

"What have you got to lose?"

I said, "He's my partner."

"Partner in love or business?"

"Both. Neither." She made the encouraging noncommittal sound practiced by headshrinkers the world over. I said, "He thinks I'm crass."

"Is he right?"

"There's nothing wrong with a little spunk." I licked salt off my palm. I could tell the word "defensive" was flashing like traffic lights in her head. I said, "I'm not being defensive."

"But you're being defensive about not being defensive."

I smirked. "He says I'm controlling."

"Is he right?"

"He can do whatever the fuck he wants." Running out on me must fit into that category. But maybe I made him do that, too.

"Do you love him?" she asked.

"No. We're partners. I've known him for too long as a friend."

"Feelings can change."

"Whatever. It doesn't matter anyway. He's gone."

"Did you try to stop him?"

"Of course not."

"Did you tell him you love him?"

"I just told you that I don't."

"Who do you love?" she asked.

I said, "I don't love anyone. I love my job."

"And how's that going?"

"Lousy. I could lose it all by Tuesday at midnight."

"Don't get down about it. Things have a way of working themselves out. Let life happen to you. Follow your own blueprint for living." A Taoist no less, this Deb.

I said, "I wouldn't talk like that in class if I were you."

"They love that shit at NYU."

I asked her to tell me more about Johann. Did he ever get a bit too frisky and try to strangle anyone?

She said, "Johann's not like that. He's straight in the sack. Just touch that guy and he'll get a ten-foot hard-on. I personally got him off five times one night. That was before he hooked up with Belle."

"About Belle," I said.

"He never got specific. He just told me he'd hit the big time with her. I think he was more cavalier than he really felt. I think he loved her."

"And you would know," I said. "Do you think Luigi might remember anything more specific?"

She said, "I don't know. But I wouldn't ask him. He's sensitive about keeping his patrons anonymous."

I said, "I'm sure Luigi is a very sensitive guy." I checked my watch. The hands spun a bit too quickly. Or maybe that was my head. It was midnight, and the Orchid was filling up. Deb couldn't help watching likely lays spilling in from Broadway. It was time for me to go. I tried standing. Didn't work. My hollow legs were pickled with worm juice. Deb came around the bar to help me, her breasts and ponytails bopping sweetly. She put an arm around my waist and walked me to the door. I said, "How much do I owe you?"

"Don't worry about it now. Pay me next time I see you. I'll hold on to the check."

"I meant for the shrink session."

"I don't think I helped you much."

"I don't feel worse than I did when I came in. Then again, I don't feel much of anything."

"On the house," she said. "For talking to me longer than five minutes and not grabbing my tits."

I told her good-bye and closed the door to the Orchid behind me. I'd forgotten about the man in the floppy hat. I staggered around Times Square in search of a working pay phone. I finally found one and called Alex at home. He picked up and said hello; I hung up immediately. I'm sure he knew it was me. I hate it when I act like a girl.

CHAPTER EIGHT

TOO MUCH DASHING AROUND WITH A HANGOVER

I called Alex first thing. He didn't seem pleased to hear from me. It was about ten Monday morning. He agreed to meet me at Do It Right in an hour. My bed stunk of tequila. I showered and doused myself with Love's Baby Soft. I got dressed—a jeans-and-sneaks day if there ever was one—and went outside. The sun blinded me. Rather, the sun helped to blind me. I was well hung over.

I prepared my apology speech on the subway. Alex and I were simply getting on each other's nerves. A tough case will do that to you. I recited my part aloud, annoying the late-morning commuters on the D train. I took my favorite seat next to the subway door—we detectives like to be as close to the exit as possible.

The sun poured into the train as it crept over the East River on the Manhattan Bridge out of Brooklyn. My eyes wandered into the next car through the window. I saw *him*—the same floppy hat that had been haunting me all over the city. I shrunk down in my seat, hoping he wouldn't see me. It occurred to me that he wouldn't be on the train unless he knew I was there anyway. I straightened up and decided to confront him. Belle had always told me to face my fears.

I waited for the train to stop at Grand Street in Chinatown, then I crossed into his car. Hurried Asians poured in, talking loudly. He didn't look my way. I walked down the aisle, stepping over grocery bags and outstretched legs. I had one hand on Mama in my purse, the other on the railing above the seats.

I was standing right in front of him when the train lurched. I stumbled backward. Just as I was about to hit the ground he caught me by the waist. Mama dropped out of my bag and slid under his seat. An old Chinese woman screamed. Every eye in the train was on my gun. The man's grip tightened. I struggled to free myself. He reached under his seat for the gun. I saw him grasp it by the handle, one finger resting against the trigger. I closed my eyes and felt lightheaded.

He shook me and said, "Hey, baby. Snap out of it." He swung me into the seat next to him. He said, "You dropped your piece." I looked at him closely and apologized. I put my gun back and tried to act nonchalant. The commuters went back to reading their papers. Only in New York. So I don't always see straight with a hangover. I should have worn my glasses.

By the time I reached 42nd Street I was steady as a cat in heat. I sped over to Do It Right, figuring Alex would be there already, waiting for me to kick-start the day's sleuthing. I had to clear up two issues with him first: that I wanted him on the case, and that I wanted him on me. I'm not sure when I made up my mind about the latter. I suspect I've known for a while—the girlfriend, colleague obstacles be damned. This is how I thought things would go:

He'd be sitting in the client comfy chair. I'd walk in and say, "Alex, first of all, I'm sorry."

He'd be humble and say, "No, Wanda. I'm sorry."

I'd say, "Alex, Alex. Always taking the blame for my indiscretions. Well, I won't let you do it this time. I did take Candie's number. I can't tell you how profoundly pathetic I feel for lying to you. And that I've run the risk of losing your trust. I don't know if I can handle that." I wouldn't manufacture the tears yet.

He'd say, "Wanda—"

I'd stop him with a raised palm and say, "No, let me finish. I also lied when I said my kiss was platonic. You must know it wasn't. In all the time we've known and respected each other, I never got the faintest hit that we might see each other as more than friends. When I found myself wanting that, I didn't know how to react. Maybe I treated you badly because of my confusion. You must understand that. Plus, I was distracted with Belle's murder and all. And by the way, Skip doesn't mean anything to me. He's just a lust outlet and a paycheck. Nothing more. You're the one I want. And I didn't realize until it was too late. I've been such a terrible person—I don't deserve you anyway."

"Wanda, don't talk about yourself that way."

"Alex, I have to start being honest with myself. I feel like an asshole for how selfish I've been. Please let me acknowledge my assholeness. I can only hope that you'll be able to forgive me. Because if you don't, I don't know what I'll do." Then the tears would gush.

"Of course I forgive you. I love you," Alex would say.

"You're too good for me."

"Nothing's too good for you." Then we'd kiss for real, without the slightest breath of anything platonic. All would be right again, and we could get on with the ratty business of ferreting out a killer.

Alex had different plans. Just as I anticipated, he was sitting in the client comfy chair when I came in. I said, "Alex, first of all, I'm sorry."

He said, "Save it. You manipulated my feelings and abused my trust. It's as simple as that. We do have a case to solve, though, and it could mean a lot of money for both of us. I assume you'll be sharing Belle's half mil with me for being your partner?" I must have misheard him.

I started again. "Alex, first of all, I'm sorry."

"I know what you're doing, Mallory. You've worked out this elaborate script, and you expect me to read along. Just like you planned for Belle the day she died, just like you plan for every emotionally sticky situation in your life. I will not play your game and slide into your trap. And I certainly won't fall all over myself accepting an insincere apology. So forget the speech. I don't want to hear a word of it. Because you don't mean a word of it."

The horrible truth was that I *did* mean most of it. I stammered for words. The phone saved me; I walked over and picked it up. It was the obscene caller. He said, "I'm watching you." I threw the phone down and froze.

Alex asked who it was. "The same random obscene caller who called me twice yesterday," I replied. Before he could respond the phone rang again.

Alex picked up the receiver and said, "Who the fuck is this?"

I watched him. He looked especially handsome that Monday. He'd done something different with his hair. It was—I don't know—shinier.

He said into the phone, "Sorry, Herb. I thought it was someone else. . . . Okay. We'll be right over." He put the receiver down and said, "Son of come balloon at *Midnight*."

"For who?"

"Cheryl."

"Let's go."

We went to *Midnight* and zipped right up to the ninth floor. Yolanda grunted a short hello to me and buzzed us through. Herb was waiting beyond the doors. He said, "Welcome. You guys missed a great party last night. Cheryl's in the ladies' room. Maybe you should help her out, Wanda."

I said, "Me? Help Cheryl? She'll love that." I walked down the familiar dusty-rose corridor to the john. Cheryl stood in her skirt and wide-band underwire bra, rinsing out her Donna Karan sweater. I hopped on the sink next to her and said, "I have a hangover, and I've had a rough morning. I don't have the energy to dance with you. Just tell me what happened." I rummaged in my purse for a cigarette, lit it, and kerplunked my bag in the next sink over.

She was frazzled. Pieces of hair stuck out of her tight bun like twigs from an old broom. She didn't look up. "No smoking," she said, and she pointed to the sign.

"You'll live." I took a drag.

She dunked her sweater and said, "Look, Wanda. You know I'm not your biggest fan. And I know you're not my biggest fan. And if I wasn't absolutely desperate, I wouldn't have had Herb call you." She paused. "Some horrid person sent me a package today. In that package was a balloon."

"On the outside of the balloon were the words 'Prick me' written with Liquid Paper. You popped the balloon, and a mixture of come and water sprayed all over your cube and all over you."

She stopped scrubbing her sweater and said, "How the hell do you know that? I specifically told Herb not to reveal any details."

"Why'd you pop it?"

"What do you mean? The instructions said to pop it."

"Belle got one just like that the day she was killed. Didn't you know?"

"No, I didn't. Could that mean—"

"Might. Might not. Was there a note in the balloon?"

"Yes."

"What did it say?"

"It said 'I came to say happy birthday.' And the peculiar thing is that it's not my birthday. What did the note in Belle's balloon say? Same thing?"

"Who picked up the package for you at Yolanda's desk?"

"I did."

"Not your assistant?"

"I don't have an assistant. She quit." I puffed my cigarette and waited for her to continue. She resumed scrubbing and said, "I bumped everyone up one notch when I took over. Except my assistant. She wanted more creative responsibilities, but she inputs so beautifully, and now that I'm editor I have so many more correspondences and appointments. And she was damn good at keeping track of all that."

"Always driving the best ones away," I said.

Her face flamed. "I don't want to hash over old business, Wanda. You are no longer associated with this magazine, and the things that go on here are none of your business." Her chest heaved.

"Well, then, I guess I'll be going." I edged off the sink. Cheryl grabbed my arm.

"You're perfectly prepared to walk out of here and let a twisted killer track me down like some defenseless rabbit in the forest, just like Belle. Please, Wanda —and I won't bother mentioning how sick it makes me to say this—I need your protection. I have to keep this quiet—my reputation is at stake. And you're the only person I know who's seedy enough to help."

"You're a defenseless bunny like I'm Betty Boop," I said.

"Don't you dare make me beg."

I wanted her to squirm. I batted my lashes. "I don't know. It's not like you've been very nice to me all these years."

She said matter-of-factly, "I can help you find Belle's murderer." I edged back on the sink and listened. She said, "Belle was sent a balloon the day she was killed, right? If the person who sent it is the killer, then he'll be after me."

"Possibly."

"I can't believe I'm bartering for my life with *you.*" She pulled the stopper in the sink and wrung out the sweater. She inspected it for stains. Finding one, she cranked the hot water and dunked the sweater again.

I said, "The balloon could be a redder herring than Stalin. Herb told me readers send you all kinds of sex gags. Like the cucumber sculpture on his desk."

"Some bondage wear, maybe a few fist-shaped vibrators. But never body fluids that could contain communicable diseases. Please, Wanda. I'm begging here. Stay with me for the next twenty-four hours. You shadow me, and maybe you'll turn up a killer."

"Frankly, Cheryl, I don't think I could get through a day with you. Especially not today."

"Can't we put away our personal differences to save my life and help you earn $500,000?"

"Or waste a whole day of the investigation."

"You carry a gun, right?"

"Yes, I do."

"And you know how to use it?"

I yanked Mama from my purse—the pearl handle gleaming in the fluorescent bathroom light. I unhooked the safety, aimed, and fired. I hit my mark, and tampons spewed out of the slot machine on the wall. I blew dramatically into the barrel and ducked Mama back inside my bag. I said, "Sure, I know how to use it."

She finally looked at me square in the eye and said, "You are seriously deranged."

"I never miss a dramatic opportunity."

"This must be a bad dream," she said gloomily. "Protect me, and I'll make it worth your while."

Bingo. That's what I wanted to hear. "Okay, Cheryl," I said. "I've got some business to take care of. Don't leave the office for any reason for the rest of the day. I'll be back at six."

"But I'm scheduled to speak at an ASME luncheon." (That's the American Society of Magazine Editors.)

I said, "If you live through lunch, I'll see you at six." She said she'd cancel. I pocketed some tampons from off the bathroom floor and left.

I met Alex in Herb's office. Herb asked about the investigation, but I didn't want to tell him too much. He asked if Cheryl was okay. I said she was. Herb fiddled with the cucumber statue on his desk. I asked him if a reader had really sent that in, or if it was a gift from Larry.

Herb laughed and confided, "Actually, Belle gave it to me for Valentine's Day."

We said good-bye to him and stopped to chat with Yolanda on the way out. She said that Stan, the sign-in man, had brought the package up, just like before. We walked out to the elevator bank.

Ginger Jones, the lily-scented staff writer, chased us down there. She looked hot as usual in a tawny knit sweater that contrasted with her long caramel hair. She smiled at me and said, "Hello, Wanda."

"Hello, Ginger."

She thrust out her hip provocatively. Alex stared. "I hear you're doing a story on Belle for Skip Giddy at *Shinola,*" she said.

One can never escape publishing-world gossip. I said, "Yeah. I'm working on it."

"I hear Skip is an attentive editor." I could tell by her smile that that wasn't all she'd heard.

I said, "He's okay." Alex grimaced.

"I've heard he's better than okay," she said with a lust-dripping smile.

The elevator finally arrived, and Alex and I stepped in. I said, "You're a good reporter, Ginger. Why don't you find out for yourself?"

As the doors closed I heard her say, "I just might do that."

We found Stan leaning on the messenger table in the lobby. His all-white uniform needed cleaning. He straightened up as we approached. I said, "Hello, Stan."

He said, "Mallory, right? I remember you from last week."

"You took another package up to *Midnight* today. Same size and wrapping as last week. Do you remember what the messenger looked like this time?"

He scratched his head and said, "Same thing. I went to visit the men's room. I came back and saw this big box sitting on my desk. Right here."

"Right here?"

"Just like that. And I brought it right up to Yolanda because I didn't get a slip for it. Just to make sure Cheryl got it."

"So you noticed it was addressed to Cheryl."

"I've got eyes, you know. I couldn't help but read it."

I said, "Of course. But one thing confuses me, Stan. When I was here last week, didn't I ask you to call me if you remembered anything, or if anything like this happened again?"

"I suppose you did," he said. "But with all the business around here with Cheryl taking over . . . all the flower deliveries . . . I forgot."

"Will you remember if there's a next time?"

"Yeah."

"You didn't happen to see a tall man in a floppy hat and overcoat hanging around here today, did you?"

He said, "Nah." I wrote the number at Do It Right on the sign-in sheet. He'd have no excuses if there was a next time.

Alex and I went straight to Gladman's office to talk to Martha about her refrigerated collection of facial ointment. It seemed to be making a big splash at *Midnight*. I told Alex on the way up Sixth Avenue to BG&B that Cheryl Stingon, dragon-lady, had begged me to be her baby-sitter. "But while I'm protecting her from the mad come-ballooner, who'll protect her from me?" I asked. Alex chuckled. It was a nice chuckle, as genuine as genuine can be. And he treated me to an adorable smile.

"So are you talking to me again?" I asked.

"I was always talking to you, Wanda."

I thought I'd give my speech another try. I said, "Alex, first of all, I'm sorry."

"You never give up, do you?"

I played dumb. "Give up what?"

"Trying to worm out of what you did with pretty words."

"I'm trying to be sincere."

"When you *are* sincere we'll talk." I started to

protest, but Alex gave me a don't-try-it look. I fumed but didn't say anything. He said, "Let's concentrate on the case, okay? We can get back to us later." I nodded. He put his arm on my shoulder. My heart leapt. I snuck a peek at him. He was smiling and looking at his shoes. There are few things as irritating as a man who knows how to wait.

We twiddled our thumbs for a few minutes in Gladman's oak-paneled office. A secretary told us that he was in conference with one of his partners; actually, we were waiting for Martha to come back from lunch. In the meantime I decided to talk to Gladman about an extension. We only had a day and a half left. Just thinking about arranging a deal revived the pounding in my skull. I felt lousy. The only thing worse than a tequila hangover is a tequila hangover with cramps.

Gladman entered and said with faux-brightness, "Ms. Mallory. Mr. Beaudine. A pleasure as always. I see you've made yourselves comfortable." We were sitting in the overstuffed French provincials. He took a seat behind his massive desk.

Alex said, "These chairs are very nice, thank you."

Gladman said, "Stuffed tight as a banana in a peel. Now, what can I do for you today?"

"The case is more complicated than we thought," I began.

"I'm sorry to hear that, Ms. Mallory."

"We need another day."

Gladman smiled at me. He said, "I had the most lovely conversation with Pete Hamill yesterday."

Shit. I said, "And how's Pete?"

"He's fine." Gladman bobbed his head—he'd played his trump card well. I wondered if that was in his job description. He said, "Now, if you don't mind, I'm expecting an important call from the coast."

I said, "The bequest is a lot of money. I can't imagine keeping all of it." I damn well could, but detecting is a give-and-take business.

"I'm sure you'll find a way," Gladman said.

"I didn't realize you were such an honorable man."

"I'm sure there's a great deal we don't know about each other, Ms. Mallory."

That was that. No deals. On to new business. I said, "We want to talk to Martha."

Gladman eyeballed me. So politeness isn't my forte.

Alex said, "What Wanda means, sir, is that we hope it isn't inconvenient to wait for Martha to get back from lunch."

Gladman said, "Is this that shoe business again? I suggest that you call her later in the afternoon. I've sent her off to do some research for me at City Hall. She won't be back for at least an hour." We thanked him and left.

Our next stop was back at Do It Right. It was midafternoon, and I had a crushing headache. I hated this blasted deadline. I looked for the man in the floppy hat by the deli, but he wasn't around. I wondered if I was imagining him. Lieutenants Dick O'Flanahey and Bucky Squirely were waiting in my office. Clearly, it was designated as a torture-me day. Dick twirled his mustache and said, from his seat at my desk, "About time. Don't you people work?" Bucky was tossing lint from his pockets out the window. I walked past them and sat down in my chair. Alex followed suit.

I made a tent with my hands. "Gentlemen, how can I help you?"

"Gentlemen?" Bucky said.

Dick said, "Come, now, Tom. It doesn't hurt to be shown a little well-deserved respect."

"Well-deserved?" Alex inquired.

Dick said, "That's what the chief of detectives is saying downtown. It seems to him, and to us, that we've got the Beatrice case all wrapped up. And"—he indulged in a self-congratulatory smirk—"Lieutenant Squirely and I will be given promotions. But you can read all about that in tomorrow's paper after the press conference."

I said, "You've pegged Johann?"

Bucky said, "You got that right." He nodded furiously.

I said, "And I suppose it doesn't matter to the gentlemen downtown that Johann's not the killer." (He could very well be, but no way was I going to let them leave without doubts.)

Dick said, "What's that smell?" He sniffed the stale office. "Do you smell sour grapes?"

"The only thing I smell is your BO," I retorted.

Dick said, "You're a smart one. But you can say anything you want, cupcake. This case is closed, according to the New York City Police Department. Some uniforms are picking up Johann Pesto as we speak. And that should mean that this case is closed for you. I guess you won't be seeing any of the Beatrice estate. And I guess that means this pathetic rinky-dink operation will close down. That's really too bad."

"Good riddance," Bucky added.

"So what solidified the case?" Alex asked.

"Wouldn't you like to know," Bucky guffawed.

Alex said, "No, really. If the case is wrapped, then what difference does it make to tell us now? We concede. We'll stop our investigation."

I said, "The hell we will."

Alex said, "We will, Wanda. The police have solved the case." He gave a humor-me look. Dick caught it.

Dick said, "That's right, honey. Let the guy speak. He's just doing his best to weasel information out of us." Alex shrugged.

I said, "If you've come here to gloat, you're past finished. So why don't you and your dickless partner blow?"

"I was just about to treat you to the story of our brilliant deduction in solving this case," Dick complained. "But if you don't want to hear it, then I guess we'll go."

"Get going, then. What are you waiting for? The Second Coming of Christ?"

"Then you won't hear the story of my mythical wisdom and my stunning ingenuity," Dick whined.

I said, "The Dalai Lama couldn't persuade me to listen to you. Besides, any bull you've concocted doesn't mean shit. Because Johann isn't the killer. And I've got plenty of evidence to prove it," I lied. Dick's face blazed behind the mustache.

Bucky said, "Yeah? Like what?"

"Wouldn't you like to know?"

Dick roared, "She's full of shit."

I said, "What, you don't want to hear the story of my mythical wisdom and stunning ingenuity?"

Dick twisted his mustache, trying to maintain control. "There you go again, not respecting the badge. And you know how much that annoys me. I'll give you a chance now to perform your duty as a public citizen and share all information with us. Or else you and your partner might have to finish this investigation from a hospital bed."

I said, "But I'm full of shit, remember?" Dick stepped toward me. I feared for a second that I'd gone too far. He stopped himself and signaled to Bucky to follow his exit. I yelled out the open door, "I'm going to that press conference tomorrow. Just see who makes the papers."

They bombed back in. Alex leapt to my side and gestured protectively. Dick poked his finger inches from my face and boomed, "This case is closed. Do you hear me?" I nodded, and they left.

The phone rang. It was the obscene caller. He said, "I'll get you today."

That was all I needed. I slumped over my desk. Alex put his hand on my shoulder. For a microsecond I wondered how bad law school could be. Alex brought me back.

"Something will give, Wanda," he said. "Something's got to give." I turned to him. The light coming in from the afternoon sun made his face look bronzed. I don't think I'd ever seen him look better. Along with his talent for stating the obvious, Alex always says the right thing.

I said, "Have I told you recently that you're an okay guy?"

"No," he said with a charming smile.

I said, "Remind me when you're due."

A few hours later we tried phoning BG&B. Martha hadn't returned, and Gladman sounded worried. I hung up and told Alex I was off to find Martha. Alex wanted to go with me, but I instructed him to find Johann at the police station. I figured Johann would be ready to talk—for the record, to use his words—after some time in the slammer.

My first stop was at Martha's building. No answer at Martha's or Johann's buzzer. I peeked in Stephanopoulos's for Cosmos, but he wasn't there. Martha was on the run—from what, I didn't know. The sun had set already, and the night air was cooler than it had been all week. I ducked into a nearby bar. The only way I'd get rid of my headache at this point was to have a drink.

I found a stool, and the bartender asked me what I needed. I said, "Hair of the dog that ravaged me." He raised an eyebrow. I said, "Margarita on the rocks is fine." So much for my on-duty vodka rule. I gulped it down and split.

The booze helped. Outside, the nip had turned cruel. I had a sweater at Do It Right in my desk drawer. I flagged down a cab and headed back uptown to see if Martha had left a message for me at the office.

I got out at Broadway. On the way up the block I glanced at my reflection in a storefront window. Strands of red hair flew out in too many directions. I braided my hair as I walked. The street was massed with people, as was usual for 9:30 on a weeknight. A tingle ran up my spine like a monkey up a rope swing. Trouble was near. I spun around. I saw no one I recognized when I looked up and down the street. I put on my glasses and looked again. Nothing.

I took my shortcut through the construction by 43rd Street. Once I was off the street the night got quiet. I felt safer then. In my rush I tripped over a two-by-four. I cursed, and I got up slowly. A voice said, "I hope you're okay." I looked around and saw no one.

"Who's there?" I asked.

He said, "I told you I get you today." The man in the floppy hat stepped into view from behind a steel pillar. It was too dark to make out his face. My heart pounded. In my haste I'd left Mama at the office.

"Who are you?"

He said, "I like your hair down better." I inched backward. My ankle hurt. I turned toward the street. No one walked past.

"I had to get it off my face." I kept inching.

He said, "Take another step and I kill you." I froze. He came closer to me. I contemplated running, but I didn't know if it was a gun in his pocket. He said, "You very pretty tonight." He took another step, and a streetlight beam hit his face. It was Cosmos.

I said, "Cosmos. Look, I've got to run. I'm late for an appointment."

He said, "I lose my job because of you."

I swallowed hard. I said, "I'm sorry. I'll help you find another one tomorrow."

"I don't want help."

I said, "I like that hat. You wear that hat a lot, don't

you? Like last Thursday night? When you attacked a brunette woman across the street from the diner? I know all about that, Cosmos. I can help you. Why don't we go up to my office and have a talk, okay?"

"No!" he shouted. "Don't talk. You talk too much. You made me look like a fool the other day. And I just wanted to go dancing."

In a flash he grabbed me by the wrists and backed me against a saw table. He said, "We dance now." He picked me up and threw me down on it. Something sharp pressed into my spine. I cried out. I struggled to get up, but he kept one hand pressed on my ribs, and the other held my wrists.

"American women think they know so much," he muttered. "They think they can do anything. Look at you now, tough lady." With one hand he unbuttoned my jeans as I struggled, and he pulled them down around my knees. Whatever poked me in the back rolled out next to me. It was a bent twelvepenny nail. Cosmos ripped my underwear. He moved his hand from my ribs to unzip his pants. He pulled his dick out. I flailed on the table and kicked my legs. He slapped me. He held his dick in his hand. He said, "You see it's true what they say about Greek men." I stopped squirming and looked. I tried to relax enough to think. I had to get out of this.

I said, "It is true." He smiled. I said, "I like it."

He said, "I know you like it. American women like big men."

"Let me touch it."

"I tell you what to do."

"Tell me to touch it."

"Touch it," he said. He let go of my hands. I gently stroked him with one hand. With the other I groped in the dark for the nail. I almost had it in my grasp when Cosmos pulled away from me. He slapped me in the face and pushed me to one side. He saw the nail. He picked it up, slapped me again, and rolled me onto my stomach.

He said, "This is what you want?" I felt a pinch on my butt. The nail broke my skin. Blood dripped down my leg. And fingers worked their way into me. So this is fear, I thought.

Suddenly Cosmos was off me. I leapt off the table, forgetting my pants were binding my legs. I fell forward. Slowly I looked up. What I saw: Cosmos pinned to the ground, a six-inch blade at his throat. I stood and pulled up my pants. My legs were a mess, scraped and chewed up from my fall. My ankle ached. I sat down on the saw table and lit a cigarette.

I said, "I thought you were in jail."

Johann didn't look up once. He ran the knife down toward Cosmos's exposed genitals. Cosmos whimpered. Johann said, "I was hiding out at the Orchid. Good thing I saw you walk by across the street. I wanted to talk to you."

"I had this guy right where I wanted him," I lied.

"If that's where you wanted him, I can recommend a good psychologist."

"Not our friend Deb at the Orchid?" I asked.

"The very same."

"And I didn't think we had any friends in common —besides Belle, of course." Johann maneuvered Cosmos to his feet. I flicked my cigarette and limped over to them. I zipped Cosmos's pants and kneed him lovingly in the nuts. He doubled over, Johann holding him by the hair.

"What do you want to do with him?" Johann asked.

"Let's take him to Do It Right. And Johann—thanks."

He smiled. Have I mentioned that Johann is gorgeous? We headed for the office, me limping and Johann dragging the crying Greek. I wanted answers from Cosmos. But hat or no hat, I had decided that he wasn't Martha's attacker. The strangler had had a different modus operandi. Not once during the attempted rape did Cosmos put his hands anywhere near my neck.

CHAPTER NINE

MISADVENTURES IN VOYEURISM

Cosmos put up a struggle, but he was no match for Johann. We tied him to my desk chair with bandage tape from the first-aid kit. He blubbered and complained that the tape ripped his arm hair. I gave him the last drops of Amaretto to calm him. It didn't work.

The phone rang. I hesitated and picked up. It was Cheryl. She'd been waiting for me at *Midnight* for hours. It was after 10:00. I told her to call a car, go home, and lock the doors. I had bigger meat to grill. She hissed that I was a two-bit sleaze broker, told me to forget about seeing any of her money, and hung up with a cheerful fuck-you.

I said, "Okay. Now that we're all comfortable, let's chat."

Johann said, "What should we do with him?"

"If we take him to the police, he'll tell them that you saved me, and men in blue will be up your ass like a billy club. If we let him go, he might come after me again. And frankly, Johann, I'm more interested in protecting my ass than yours."

"What are you proposing?" Johann asked.

"Let's make a deal." I lit a cigarette. "I need information. You need to stay covered. Start talking."

"Just for the record," he said, "I think you owe me more than petty extortion. I did save you from a potentially damaging situation."

Indeed he did. I said, "Start by telling me who you've been screwing these days. Cheryl Stingon, perhaps?"

Johann stared blankly at me. "Cheryl who? I never heard of any Cheryl."

"Sorry, Johann," I said. "She was at the funeral, and the will reading, and she was a big part of Belle's life. You know damn well who Cheryl is. Come to think of it, I remember seeing the two of you schmoozing merrily away at the funeral." Johann gave me a confused look. I inhaled some smoke and said, "We could sit here for hours going back and forth, not getting anything done, leaving depressed, and feeling in general like poop. Or you could try trusting me. You don't have much to lose at this point."

Johann fidgeted in his seat. Finally he said, "Cheryl and I have been seeing each other. Just a few dates. No big deal."

"Does Martha know?"

"Of course."

"Why does she put up with it?"

"You'll have to ask her that."

"I would, but no one knows where she is." Johann's blue eyes bugged. So he didn't know. I said, "She's been missing since this morning. Went out to lunch and never came back."

"We've got to find her," he said urgently. He seemed to think there was something to worry about.

"So the attack Thursday night was for real."

He snapped, "Of course it was for real. Why would we make that up?"

There was a whole fistful of reasons why, but I let it go. I said slowly, "As soon as we finish here, we'll find her. Okay?" He breathed deeply and agreed. Cosmos had stopped wrestling with the chair and was watching us closely. I didn't think he understood much of the English.

"Why didn't Martha mind you sleeping with other women?" I asked.

"It's not that she didn't mind. It's a physical necessity. I need sex five times a day."

"Johann, you knave."

"I wish I were just bragging. I've got a disease called semenintasis. I'm allergic to my own semen. My body produces a certain amount each day, and I have to evacuate it from my system, or I have epileptic-like fits. If I don't, or can't, I'll die. The only known cure is castration. And I won't do that. About ten years ago there was another case of semenintasis documented here in the U.S. A doctor in New York has been studying the disease since then. He's the only one who's made any progress. I came here to meet him and let him use me for medical experimentation. That's why I went to an American school in Stockholm—my parents knew all hope was here, with Dr. Martin. But we haven't had any luck. Yet. That's why I'm running from the police. I have nothing to hide about the murder—I'm innocent, and that will become evident. But if I get put in jail, I'll be dead in a day." He added bitterly, "I doubt the police would file women through my cell every few hours."

I remembered Deb telling me she got him off five times in one night. "Will masturbation work?" I asked.

He said, "I can't get a hard-on by myself. And believe me, I've tried."

"What happened the night we met at the Orchid Lounge?" I asked.

"That was Martha's idea. After Belle died, Martha tried to take care of me by herself. It worked for a day or two, but then she got tired. She still didn't want me to see other women alone, so she suggested a threesome. We planned to give it a run at the Orchid. And we met you. It didn't work, though; I needed more. We had to leave there after you did and go back to my place."

I didn't know what to say. Should I be insulted? Johann said, "All my life I've had to endure forced fucking. Like a diabetic eating at specific times, I've had to fuck a specific amount each day. I don't even enjoy it anymore."

"Really?" Cosmos chimed in. I guess he understood more than I thought.

"Maybe a little," Johann admitted. "But I'll never have a normal relationship. I'd have to cheat. For the record, I did plan to marry Belle. With her money, I thought I'd be able to speed along the medical research. Martha didn't want me to marry Belle, but she wanted me to get cured. It was, as you Americans say, a catch-22 situation for her." He stroked his chin pensively. He said, "I suppose I took advantage of Belle. But I felt justified because of my disease. Also, she made it easy. Martha and I met at our building when I moved in. Before then I spent all my money on prostitutes at the Orchid. I met Belle at BG&B when I was there to pick up Martha after work. Belle asked me to dinner, and we made love that night. And the rest is history."

"And Belle knew about your, um, condition?"

"No. I was going to explain that once we were married. If I'd known Belle was having me investigated, I would have told her sooner. Or you would have."

I said, "Shit, all I came up with were vibrating eggs." I'd had no clue about his disease. How could I have? Guilt took me over. I remembered all the times I slacked off on my investigation of Johann. I might have taken advantage of Belle, too.

Johann said, "Belle didn't love me. I was a plaything for her."

"I don't know about that."

"But Martha really loves me. She'd do anything to help me."

"And the come in the fridge, that's yours, right?"

"Samples for Dr. Martin." If he was telling the truth, it all made sense, and it seemed to clear Johann. But not Martha. My cigarette had burned down to the filter. I let the ash fall on the orange carpet, and I stepped on it. Alex would kill me if he saw that.

"How jealous would you say Martha is?" I asked.

"Pretty jealous, but she understands the need."

"Jealous enough to kill?"

He shook his head violently, his blond mane flying. "No way. She's not capable of it. And besides, she was with me when Belle died."

"The two of you have lied plenty already covering for each other."

"I'm telling the truth," he pleaded. I wasn't convinced.

"Would Martha send Belle and Cheryl balloons full of your come to scare them?"

He said, "That's impossible. She knows those samples are important for research. She wouldn't waste a drop." But there were plenty more drops where those came from.

"What do you know about those poems?"

"Nothing other than that Belle got some also and thought they were from me. I denied it, but she didn't believe me. Actually, Martha didn't get any poems until Belle was dead." He turned a bit gray. "We've got to find Martha. Those poems may be the connection." Johann twitched. I figured he might need to evacuate a helping of love juice.

The issue of Cosmos was at hand. I walked over to him, taped down in my chair. He wasn't scared anymore, so I slapped him across the face. I decided to reason with him.

I said, "Cosmos. This is your choice. I take you to the cops and turn you in for attempted rape. If you talk about my friend Johann, he will be joining you in jail, and he'll tear you apart for setting him up—I think you know he can." Cosmos looked over at Johann and his large Swedish frame. I continued, "Option two: We let you go. But first Johann takes his knife and slices your big Greek dick down the middle like a hot dog to guarantee you won't bother me again. Your decision. You've got five seconds."

He took one. I taped his wrists behind his back and took him to the station by cab. Cosmos and I told the cops that he had tried to rape me, and I overcame him alone. They booked him, and that was that. Johann was to remain in hiding at the Orchid Lounge. I took the responsibility of finding Martha. Johann wanted to help, but I wouldn't let him. I couldn't risk his getting caught and twitching to death of semenintasis in prison. He might be needed on the outside later.

Tuesday, October 22, 1:00 P.M. The last day in my week-long killer quest—just eleven hours from deadline. Alex and I shared a pot of coffee (of all days to evoke strength through java, I needed it now) at Do It Right while I told him what had happened with Cosmos and Johann. He'd spent the night getting the runaround from the cops. None would admit that Johann was at large. It was damper than it had been all month. My hair frizzed. Indian summer was finally rolling into autumn, and I welcomed it. I filled my mug for the third time. Alex said, "Jesus, Wanda. Give it a rest." There was still no sign of Martha.

Herb called first thing. Cheryl hadn't shown for work and hadn't called in sick. He'd tried to reach her at home, but he got the machine. I figured she was there safe, too scared to leave or answer the phone. I told Herb to relax and hung up.

Santina also called. She had big news and wanted to come over. I told her to forget it, that we were busy. She said, "Great, I'll be over in a few hours."

The phone rang one more time. It was Gladman. He

asked if I'd had any luck finding Martha. I said that I hadn't. He asked me to please keep trying.

I lit my first cigarette of the day.

A few hours later Alex and I decided to break for food after too much futile brainstorming about the identity of our licentious poet. I suggested that he pick something up while I ran an errand. He looked at me oddly, not understanding why I'd waste time on errands on our last day, especially considering how grave things looked. I, of course, wasn't really going to pick up my dry cleaning. But Alex couldn't be privy to my secret agenda.

I hopped a downtown bus. The way things were going, Do It Right Detectives could very well crash and burn within eight hours. I hadn't given up on the $500,000, and wouldn't while there was a drop of detecting blood swimming in my body, but I wanted to insure my safety net. Even a $500 whore will roll for fifty on a rainy day.

The bus stopped at East 14th Street, *Shinola* magazine territory. I cut through the farmer's market in Union Square Park and bought a mackintosh apple to eat on the run. Skip Giddy's office is on the twentieth floor of the Paragon Building on East 16th Street. I fluffed my hair in the elevator and hurriedly applied lip color on the walk down the corridor to *Shinola*. The editorial office is usually bustling and frenetic, with copy editors screeching across the room to fact checkers, and editors deftly lying about late checks to hysterical writers. But that evening no one was around. I remembered that this was ASME lecture week. Cheryl was supposed to have spoken the day before. The editor of *Shinola* probably had the honors that Tuesday, and the loyal staff must have gone to hear him. I slid past the front desk, watched the switchboard flash for a second, and decided what to do. Skip would appreciate a dirty little note. I sat at the switchboard and scribbled a suggestive yet discreet letter. I folded it three ways and (nauseating, I know) sealed it with a kiss.

I was halfway back to Skip's office when I smelled lilies. My aggravatingly accurate sense of smell signaled trouble. I inched open Skip's door and saw them. Buck-ass naked. Ginger was spread like a wishbone on Skip's desk. Skip hovered over her like the Spider-Man float in the Macy's Thanksgiving Day Parade. Reflexively I jumped back. I leaned against Skip's assistant's desk in the main room. Then it occurred to me that I might be getting screwed. I looked again. Ginger moved like a pro, Skip like a pile driver. I walked inside. I closed the door loudly. Ginger let out a particularly enthused moan, so they didn't hear it. They gasped together, and Skip collapsed on her. She opened her eyes and saw me standing like an idiot at the door.

I said, "Hello." Ginger screamed. Skip jumped off her and faced me.

Skip said, "Wanda. Did we have a dinner date?" His dick was still hard.

"Get her out of here," Ginger said through clenched teeth. She slid off the desk and hid behind Skip.

I said, "Sorry to ruin your afterglow." Ginger muttered curse words. I said, "I want to sign a contract for the Belle piece. I've written a thousand words already. It's good, Skip. I know you'll love it," I lied.

Ginger said, "Can't you see we're busy? Jesus, you are such a lowlife."

Skip patted Ginger apologetically on the thigh. He glanced apologetically at me. He said, "Wanda, this isn't a good time." He turned back to Ginger and asked, "Can you leave us alone for a second?"

"I'm not going out there naked," she hissed.

"Just for a second," Skip said, and he whispered something in her ear. She left, but none too pleased. Skip slipped on his pants. He said, "I'm glad you came by, Wanda. I've been meaning to talk to you. About Ginger . . ."

I said, "It's none of my business."

"Just listen. I've got to say this before I chicken out."

"The last time you said that to me, I slid your pole all night." I remembered how good it felt. My emotions betrayed me. A few tears fell out of my eyes.

"Honey-bunny, don't cry," Skip said in his nauseating way.

"I'm not crying for you. I'm crying for my ego. Just give me a contract, and I'll get out of here."

"I mentioned to you that the bandleader was worried about you writing the Belle story. He's worried you won't make the deadline."

I said, "These thousand words will blow your mind, Skip."

"I'm sure they will. I'd love to read what you've got and give you comments, but I'm really just a worker bee here, Wanda. What the bossman wants, he gets. I pitched hard for you."

In a pig's eye, I thought. "I'm not going to grovel, Skip. You know this is my story."

"Ginger knew Belle as well as you did. And she's a more responsible reporter."

This deadline curse was breaking me. "Okay. What do you want?"

"Nothing. It's over. But not between us, I hope. You know how much I want you, angel." With unspeakable gall he came over to me, gripped my ass, and kissed me. He pulled away, gave me the intense love look that had once melted my innards, and patted me on the head like Rover. He said, "I'll call you tonight. Promise. We can go to Fanelli's for dinner and then over to my place for some romping." He put his shirt on while I stared, speechless. He said, "By the way, any interviews you've done for the story? Ginger would like to hear the tapes." He sat behind his desk and arranged papers.

So that was it. I hadn't moved an inch. He smiled brightly and asked if there was anything else. Bile rose in my throat, and I fought to keep it down. I noticed Ginger's clothes piled on the floor.

I said, "I am different than the thousands of other women you've fucked."

He said, "Of course you are, bunny."

I smiled smugly and picked up Ginger's clothes. I rubbed her tawny silk blouse on my cheek. Then I walked to the window and tossed everything out onto East 16th Street. Skip leapt to the window and looked out. I hit a woman with shopping bags. I laughed. She looked up and yelled, "It's only funny till someone loses an eye." I walked out as Ginger slipped in. She screamed, and I heard Skip trying to calm her down.

She's right; I *am* a lowlife. But at that moment, I wouldn't have wanted to be anything else.

Santina was at Do It Right when I got back. She sat on my desk in her Indian summer mink with her nyloned legs crossed, munching carrot sticks from a sandwich bag. Alex sat across from her. She said, "Ugh. Didn't I tell you that coral is not your lip color?"

I said, "Santina, I told you we're busy."

Alex said, "She's just here for a second."

Santina reached over and tousled Alex's hair. She said, "Darling. You two should get married." Alex and I both blushed.

I was losing my patience. "Can you please make this quick, Santi?" I asked. "We're trying to nab a killer here."

"You should be writing those law school applications. But forget that for now. I've got some wonderful news. I know you'll die when you hear this. It's not like you get to spread this kind of news more than six times in a lifetime. Even you, Ms. Marriage Is Not a Part of My Future, will love this." She said, "Shlomo and I are getting married."

"That's wonderful, Santina!" Alex said.

I said, "About time."

"Isn't it simply fabulous?" Santina continued. "He came back from sailing last night. I said to him, 'Shlomo, did you fool around with that frosted punchboard?' And he says to me, 'Don't be silly, Santina.' So I said to him, 'Shlomo, let's get hitched.' And he said okay."

"Have you set a date?" Alex asked.

"No, no, darling. Deciding to do it is one thing. Deciding when is another. I've got to get used to the idea first. And believe you me, a girl my age deserves a long engagement."

"Girls your age usually wait a whole week," I commented.

Santina laughed and said, "Now, Wanda. You don't know how old I really am anyway." She's right. I've always guessed somewhere in the early fifties, but makeup wiz that she is, I could be wrong.

I said, "I hope you'll make room for us at the wedding."

"Are you kidding? You're my best girl. And don't say no, or I'll sit on you. Now give me one of those ciggies." I gave her one, and she walked away from Alex to enjoy the smoke. She said, "I don't know if I should wear white or not. This is my first marriage and all, and everyone deserves to wear white at least once in her life. Wanda, you're coming shopping with me at Saks tomorrow. And I won't take no for an answer. This silly case will be over by then, and it's about time you got to see a wedding dress, even if it's not yours. Maybe you'll try on a few anyway, just for fun. This marriage thing is so infectious. I want everyone to get hitched. I've already decided on the menu. Nothing too heavy, since there'll be dancing. A gigantic fruit sculpture would make a nice centerpiece, don't you think? Grapes, melons, raspberries, the whole spectrum of citrus. You name the fruit, it'll be there. And veggies. An avalanche of veggies. Crudités up the wazoo."

She rambled on, but I'd tuned her out. Something was buzzing in my head. I picked up the poems on my desk and perused: corn-silk hair, raisin nipples, wine-grape eyes, melon ass, celery ankles, raspberry lips. A veritable produce aisle of erotica. But that wasn't the big revelation. No. I was thinking about something someone had said. I could hear his voice: "Ms. Mallory, you look plump as a Jersey tomato." At the will reading, saying Cheryl "sprang like bamboo shoots." At his office, commenting that the French provincial was stuffed tight as "a banana in its peel." I couldn't be sure he was the poet. Or, for that matter, that the poet was the killer. But I was halfway out the door to find out when the phone rang.

Santina stopped me. "Where the hell do you think you're going, Ms. An Engagement Is No Big Deal? I'm not finished with the menu." Alex noticed something in my eyes. He stood up and grasped me by the shoulders.

"What is it?" he said. "What do you know?"

The phone continued to ring. When the machine picked up we heard a woman's voice. The timbre was distorted with terror. "He's coming," she said. We heard the sound of metal against metal. Then the first honest, bloodcurdling scream I've ever heard in my life. Death hung in it. I picked up the receiver, but the line was dead, too. We remained motionless for a beat. Santina spoke first.

She said, "I don't know who that was, and I hope I never meet her. But you'd better go to her, Wanda. Now." A different tune for Santi, ushering me into danger. The urgency of a death rattle does that to people.

I didn't move. I didn't know who the caller was. There were only two options, really—Martha or

Cheryl. Cheryl was the less likely, but at least we knew where to find her. Martha, my pick, was still missing. We could go to Cheryl's place to check on her, but by doing that we might lose any chance of saving Martha. And vice versa.

Alex said, reading my mind, "We've got to split up."

"You take Cheryl," I said. "I might have a lead to Martha." The words were no sooner out of my mouth than we were out the door. Santi stayed at Do It Right by the phone. Alex went uptown by cab. I ran as fast as a smoker can to the Orchid.

Deb, cute as a button in her ponytails, was mixing and matching behind the circular bar. I ran up to her, out of breath. She smiled widely at me and inquired as to my pleasure. I said, "Johann Pesto."

She looked at me strangely. He'd obviously instructed her to keep quiet. "I told you the other night that I haven't seen him in a while," she said.

"I know he's here. He knows I know he's here." She licked her lips, considering. I said, "Tell him Martha is in danger." She could tell by my tone that I wasn't fooling. She ran into the back room and stayed there for way too long. The wait made me crazy. And, as I've said, patience isn't something I've got a lot of.

I stormed through the afternoon Orchid crowd into the red-velvet-walled back room. The mirror ball slowly rotated, reflecting pink dots from the spotlight on the ceiling. A giant Day-Glo neon sculpture of an erection filled one corner. I burst into three closetlike annexes (not making myself popular with the hourly residents) before I found Johann. He was sprawled on a king-size futon in a purple cubicle with three women licking various body parts. Deb watched from the far wall. She noticed my entrance first and stated an apology to me. Apparently Johann was more interested in what the girls were doing to him than in chatting with me.

I said, "Hey. Johann. Hey." He didn't look up. I said, "Johann. Hey. Martha is in danger." I waved my arms.

He glanced my way with the same pleasure-pain expression he wore when I was at the Orchid for the first time. He smiled at me and said dreamily, "Wanda. Join us." And I kept him out of jail for this.

I said, "Hey, come boy. Some plainclothes are in the next room."

Johann finally paid full attention. He pushed the girls aside and sat up. "I don't mean to ignore you, Wanda," he said. "It's just that I happen to know Martha is okay. I spoke to her an hour ago. She's safe."

"She called me ten minutes ago. She's in trouble!"

"What did she say?"

"She didn't say anything. Just exhaled the most convincing death scream I've heard this side of the Bates Motel."

"The Bates Motel? Where's that?"

I said, "Forget it. Just tell me where she is. She could be dying!"

He said, "You're serious."

"No, I came here in a fit just to watch you jam."

He jumped up and started to dress. "She's hiding on the storage floor of our building," he said. "The thirteenth floor."

I started out. I called back to him. "Take your clothes off, sailor. The cops are probably staking out your place looking for you. It won't help me to have you around. And when this is wrapped, I'm going to find this Dr. Martin. If your story is hooey, I advise you and your defective semen to get out of this town before you lose another drop."

I hailed a cab and tooled to 123 East 31st Street. There was only one plainclothes hovering by the entrance of the building. "I was sent by Detectives Dick O'Flanahey and Tom Squirely," I said as I ran up to the building. I flashed my P.I. license, but the cop grabbed my arm.

"Forget it, babe," he said. "No one is seeing that apartment unless I get word. If you want to file a complaint, Dick and Tom are across the street at the diner."

When I sprinted into Stephanopoulos's the woman I'd pulled Mama on ducked into the bathroom and slammed the door. Dick and Bucky looked up at me. As I approached them Dick twirled his mustache and said, "If I saw you coming, I'd have to run to the can, too." He engulfed some lemon meringue.

I said, "If you boys want to make your chief of detectives happy, you'll follow me to the storage floor of Johann's building. No time for questions. Just do it."

They looked at each other. And at me. They were smart enough to know I meant it. Dick said seriously, "What's the deal?"

"It's the biggest break so far. Now, please, Martha Schpreckenspiel could be dying." I didn't even know if they knew who Martha was, and what she nad to do with the case. But with homicide dicks, the mere mention of death jet-propelled them off their stools and across the street, me in tow.

The elevator was the old and rickety kind with cage doors. It might have been faster to run the thirteen flights. On the ride I said, "How'd the press conference go, boys?" They both darkened.

Bucky said, "Canceled until we get our hands on Pesto." I thought of the other hands on Johann and had to laugh.

Dick said, "You don't get the last laugh yet, cupcake. According to my watch, you've only got five hours left. And if this is some crap just to get inside this building, I'll tear your lungs out."

Finally we reached thirteen. I pulled back the cage door to an open space, bicycles and boxes full of junk everywhere. We raced around, but there was no sign of Martha. Dick started in on me, saying he was going to have my P.I. license revoked. Bucky sat down on a trunk and started picking his teeth with his ever-ready paper clip. I noticed the lid bounce a bit when he sat. I ran to him, pulled him off, and threw back the top.

Dick stopped hollering, and we looked inside. Dick said, "Tom, get an ambulance."

I said, "I bet this phone works, but don't touch it without—" Too late. Bucky grabbed the receiver of the wallphone and went to work. Any fingerprints on it were gone. We didn't dare touch the body. Martha's face was almost blue, and the bruises around her neck could only mean one thing. The strangler had struck again.

CHAPTER TEN

MORE SATISFACTION THAN PLIANT SURRENDER

Beth Shalom Hospital is on the Upper East Side. The paramedics took Martha there via ambulance. Dick, Bucky, and I followed in their police vehicle. Dick drove, Bucky sat in back. He complained, but Dick said since it was my collar, I'd sit up front. No one drilled me about how I knew Martha was dead or dying right under their noses.

Martha was admitted to the emergency room. We had no idea about her insurance or her next of kin. I almost told them to call Alan Gladman at BG&B but thought better of it. If my hunch was right, he already knew Martha was in trouble and wouldn't want to help.

She wasn't dead, by the way. She was in an oxygen-deprivation-induced coma. None of the doctors could predict when she'd come out, if ever.

I ran to beat Dick to the pay phone, called Alex, and quickly filled him in about Martha. He'd figured out for himself about Gladman and told me he'd gotten some interesting info. Twenty minutes later he was waiting for me in front of the hospital in a cab. I jumped in. "So where is Gladman?" I asked.

"I called his office, and no one picked up," Alex said.

"Shit." I checked my watch. It was ten o'clock, only two hours from deadline.

"But he might be there," Alex said. "I got hold of his wife when I was calling around. She says he sleeps there a lot. They're getting a divorce. An ugly one. It seems Gladman has some trouble in the love department."

On the ride to West 57th Street Alex also told me what had happened when he went to Cheryl's. When he got there she'd locked herself in the bathroom of her apartment. The super let him in after Alex told him some story about being her brother, and that Cheryl was having paranoid delusions because he had forgotten to bring her medication. The super believed it, mainly because Cheryl had been acting hysterical since the night before. They broke into the bathroom. After she came at them with a Water Pik, they tackled her and tied her to the bed with a bathrobe cord. Finally alone with her, Alex managed to settle her down with pretty words, a fifth of Jack Daniel's, and a five-second back rub, at which he is expert.

After hearing all this I said, "Honey, when this is all over I'm going to buy you a car."

"Honey?" he asked.

"Would you prefer babe?"

He smiled and held my hand. We pulled up to the

BG&B building. We rode up to seven. Gladman's office door was locked, so Alex got on his knees with his specialty set and picked away. We were in.

Thank God Gladman was there, asleep in his three-piece and specs on the couch. We turned on the army of lamps one by one. By the time we'd finished, Gladman was awake. He wasn't groggy for long. He said, "What is the meaning of this?"

I said, "Sorry to wake you, sir. But we've found Martha." I looked for something in his eyes—hesitation, guilt, anything. They were too hard to see behind those Coke bottles.

He motioned us to sit in our favorite provincials. He sat behind his desk. He said, "Is she all right? I've been worried sick."

Alex said, "I'm afraid she's dead, sir. Found strangled to death in her building." A brilliant job. If I didn't know otherwise, I would have bought it, too. Gladman collapsed on his desk instantly and sobbed.

When he recovered he took off his glasses and wiped his eyes. He said, "I was extremely fond of her."

I said, "We know, sir."

Gladman rubbed his brow and said, "Yes, well, I'll be fine. Can you give me a moment?" He buried his face in his hands. We waited. After a minute he said, "I've never been much of a religious man, but when something tragic like this happens to someone close to you it makes you wonder if there's some kind of divine plan. If this was meant to happen. If Martha's time had come to join God in heaven."

I said, "Makes you wonder, sir."

"It's solace, you see," Gladman said.

"Solace, you bet."

He said, "The newspapers seem to think that this Pesto character killed Belle. Do you think he killed Martha also?" His voice cracked.

Alex said, "Actually, sir, we hoped you could tell us a bit more about your relationship with Martha."

He looked at his watch. Gladman said, "I'd prefer if we had this conversation tomorrow. I'd like to be alone now with my grief."

Alex said, "Well, sir, as you know, we have less than an hour left to crack the case, and we just can't wait until tomorrow."

He regarded Alex quizzically and said, "Good God, man. A woman is dead." He could tell by our expressions that we weren't going to leave. He said, "Fine, then, savages. I have nothing to hide. She was a loyal assistant to me for over a year. We came to be friends as well. She was a lovely woman. Faithful, proper. And she devised a brilliant color-coded filing system for me. A true gem, a plum, the pick of the apple barrel."

I said, "A peach."

Gladman said almost frenetically, "Yes. She was a real peach."

Alex said, "And I couldn't help noticing her lips like plump raspberries."

I said, "Or her eyes like wine-grapes."

Alex said, "Or her ankles like celery stalks." Gladman's mouth formed odd shapes, as if he were practicing lip-reading exercises.

He stated finally, "Yes. She had all that. But we don't need to continue this little farce, do we? Obviously you have discovered some poetry of mine. Quite good, isn't it? I'd given those poems to Martha to type neatly so I could present them to my wife on Valentine's Day. I'm an incurable romantic, you see. Hopelessly in love with my wife."

Alex said, "Forgive me, sir, but hopeless romantics don't usually sue for divorce. Besides that, all the poems were addressed as 'Odes to Martha.'"

Again Gladman moved his lips. He stood and proclaimed with evangelic passion, "This is an outrage. How dare you people come into my office and demand explanations about things that do not concern you? Fine, just . . . fine. If you must know, I did write those poems to Martha. I don't know how you people got your grubby hands on them, but I suppose that doesn't really matter now. She never knew I was the poet. And I didn't intend for her to find out. I couldn't contain my admiration for such a fine specimen of womanhood, so I hastily and passionately took pen to paper to chronicle my unbridled love for her. Even uncouth scalawags like yourselves must understand uncontrollable and irrepressible love. Love that must be expressed, regardless of the risk. I took that risk, and I'm proud. Proud of the fruits of the love that were plucked ripe from the vine, as tender poems, offerings of joy for sharing her mere presence with me. But now you people have cheapened that love by casting your greedy eyes upon it. You've made it tawdry, sullied, disgraced. You've destroyed one of the happiest periods of my life—my life as a poet in the tradition of the great bard himself. But now, now that you people have sullied my work, the bard himself would turn away in disgust for the cheapening of the muse." He fell to his knees and wept. Alex and I nodded at each other and applauded.

I said, "Bravo, sir. And the 'Odes to Belle'? Bard love there, too, huh?"

Alex said, "By the way, sir, where were you last Monday night between ten and midnight?"

Tear splotches on his face, Gladman crumpled all out on the floor. He said, "I, uh, must be more affected by Martha's death than I thought. Please leave me now. I can't answer any more questions."

Alex said to me, "Say Martha isn't dead."

I said, "Martha isn't dead."

Gladman looked up, without glasses, from the floor. He said, "Martha is alive? She can't be alive." As soon as the words were out he tried to suck them back in.

I said, "Jesus, Gladman. I'm embarrassed for you. You fell for the oldest trick in the book." I was shocked that it had worked.

He said, "How dare you people deceive me so! Vermin, filth."

I said, "Confess, sinner. If we do this nicely, I won't have to shoot you."

Gladman moved fast. He reached under his desk for the gun hidden there—a .38 police special. He stood and began firing.

I had Mama out in a flash and rolled under the desk. Alex got hit, but I couldn't tell where. I just saw the blood splatter on the arm of the provincial. Gladman's gun roar stopped suddenly, and it got quiet.

My .22 was nothing compared to his gat. He could finish me with one shot, where I might need a few. So I didn't shoot at his feet as I watched them circle the desk around to my side. I'd be lying if I said everything happened so fast, I didn't have time to think. I did. In those three seconds I thought plenty. About Belle and his fingers around her neck. About Martha. About how he tried to gyp me out of a day in the investigation just to protect himself. I even directed my anger at Cosmos toward him.

I could see him now, standing by Alex, who was unconscious in the chair. Gladman seemed to have kept his wits about him. He squinted at me, prone under the desk. My gun was pointed at his head; he rested his on Alex's temple.

He said, "I have no intention of dying alone, Ms. Mallory."

"No one has to die."

"I'm afraid that's not possible."

"Alex could be dead already," I said. "Why waste another bullet on him?" A huge lump caught in my throat. It wasn't until I said it that I realized it could be true.

"I'm impressed with your generosity, Ms. Mallory."

"Before we start shooting, tell me why you did it."

"Why, you ask?" he said. "Why would a man like me blow out the brief candle of Belle's life? Let me explain something to you, missy. I had a reputation. I had friends. I had a job. Somewhere along the way I suddenly had a wife. That woman transformed over the years into the monster she is today. She completely deadened the loins of inspiration. Deadened them to a mass of squashed yams. For her or any other woman.

"But that doesn't matter now. I didn't kill Belle because I thought she was my wife, or because I hated women, or because I hated her. What I couldn't live with was how much I hated myself because of her. And Martha."

Gladman pressed the barrel into Alex's temple and said, "So you see, Ms. Mallory, killing sometimes has to do with love."

I said, "You got that right," and unloaded five shots in rapid succession into his face. He didn't even see it coming. He should have worn his glasses.

I checked my watch as I called 911. The time: 11:53.

I spent the night in jail. I shared my cell with two working girls with purple lipstick named Lola and Besta. Nice girls. They smelled of much sex and little bathing. They asked me what I'd done. I told them I killed a lawyer. They gave me the bottom bunk and an extra blanket.

This is what happened. The cops and an ambulance arrived at BG&B. After Alex and Gladman were rushed to Beth Shalom I told the cops I had shot Gladman in self-defense. They took me downtown to make a statement. It turned out that their stenographer's water broke, and she had to leave to birth her baby. When the cops tried to videotape my statement the camcorder jammed. It was getting late. I told them to find Dick O'Flanahey and Tom Squirely. They said okay and put me in a holding cell in the meantime. Self-defense or not, they couldn't have me running the streets with a smoking gun, could they? Or at least that's what they said. I called Santina with my quarter. She said, yes, she'd get dressed and go to the hospital and find out what she could about Alex and Martha. I took great satisfaction in telling her that the strangler was a lawyer. I passed out and dreamed about baseball. I'd never killed anyone before.

When I woke up, Lola and Besta were clanking the cell bars asking for a light from Gertie, the cell-block monitor. I instinctively reached to the cement floor for my bag. I remembered it wasn't there. I told the girls to shut up. I had a raging headache. They glanced at me for half a second and resumed clanging. I closed my eyes and tried to think. The pen monitor finally brought over a light. I bummed a butt from Lola. My first cigarette in jail. It tasted swell.

At around eleven there was a commotion in the cell block. The monitor was bringing in a visitor. All the girls in the adjoining cells made catcalls and whistled as she escorted him down. I could hear him saying, "I wouldn't even stick my dick in that mouth to shut you up" on the walk down to my birdcage. He was ushered into my cell and said, "Top of the morning to you, cupcake. Nice face. I've seen puke on the street that's looked better." It was Dick. My savior.

I said, "Tell me about Alex."

He said, "Hit in the shoulder. In and out. Nearly blew his arm off, but the docs say he'll be all right. He's in post-op at Beth Shalom now. When he comes to, they'll send him home."

"Martha?"

"Came out of the coma and ID'd Gladman." He paused. "He's dead, by the way." I figured.

"So Johann is free."

"Put up quite a fight when we found him and brought him in. Had a seizure or some shit. We let him go this morning. He was gray and twitching all over."

"When do I get out?" I asked.

"What, and leave all this?" He laughed, and his mustache spread to his ears. He said, "Anytime, sweetheart. Could have sprung you last night."

"And I stayed here anyway."

"I thought it might do you some good."

"How thoughtful of you. Remind me to put roses on your grave." He almost grinned but didn't dare.

He said, "Okay, cupcake. You won. But at least you made losing interesting." His was an expression of grudging respect. It was genuinely big of him. I guess keeping me locked up was his way of initiating me.

We went to the claims desk together, and I collected my purse and gun. It felt good to hold Mama again.

I cabbed straight to Beth Shalom. By the time I got there Alex had already been discharged.

I called BG&B from the visitors' lounge. I wanted to know about the bequest. Emily put me through to Mr. Blonder, one of the partners. I said, "Emily says you've taken over the Beatrice estate from Gladman."

Blonder said, "Yes, Ms. Mallory." Icy, babe. So I'm not too popular at BG&B.

I said, "When do I see some money?"

He said, "If you are referring to the bequest, you won't be seeing any. I'm sorry, Ms. Mallory. I've already started working on payment plans for the New York Public Library and the Historical Society."

I said, "Check with 911. They recorded my call. I got Gladman before midnight. Call them. I had seven minutes."

He said, "I've conferred with my remaining partner

on this, Ms. Mallory. We know you killed my dear friend and trusted colleague before your deadline, but there was no solid proof he had anything to do with the killing until Martha Schpreckenspiel identified him as the strangler at two this morning. Two hours after deadline. I don't want to get into the complexities of this at the moment—it will be forwarded to you in writing—but basically, you won't see one red cent, you murderous bitch."

He hung up on me. I wondered for a second if I had any legal grounds on which to fight, and then I forgot about it. I wasn't that surprised that I didn't get the money. I was surprised, however, that I wasn't too disappointed.

I went looking for Alex.

I found him in his Delancey Street apartment, asleep on his good arm. His bad arm was in a sling. I didn't want to wake him. I figured he was doped and wouldn't be able to get up anyway. I left a quick note on his refrigerator pad that said he should come to dinner at my place at 8:00 P.M. and that we didn't get the money. I also wrote I was glad to see him alive.

I subbed it to the agency. There was a message from Skip Giddy. He said that he'd heard what happened and was able to convince his editor to let me do the piece after all. I called him back and told him I'd rather be force-fed ten pounds of gristle. I figured that with all the publicity I'd get for nailing Gladman, my detecting services would be the hot ticket of the month.

I spent the early evening at Do It Right, breaking in a new bottle of Amaretto and considering whether or not to buy a bigger gun, when the messenger came. He gave me an envelope. I signed for it, and he left. There was a note and a check for $30,000. The note read: "Dear Wanda—Thank you for catching Belle's killer. He got what he deserved. Accept this check as our gift to you. Please come back to Greenwich when you have the time. Sincerely, Anne and Bradley Beatrice." Not half a mil, but certainly worth the week's sweat. And enough to keep Do It Right afloat for a long time.

Martha left the hospital a few weeks later. She suffered no brain damage. According to the doctors, the strength of her neck muscles saved her. Johann confided to me later that they got so strong from giving him blow jobs every morning. When she was well enough to talk, she admitted that she was the come ballooner. She had to seek revenge on Johann's other lovers somehow. The teary confession resulted in a marriage proposal and Johann's promise of fidelity. Speaking of which, Johann's disease checked out. Although Dr. Martin sees no cure in the near future, the good doctor designed what he affectionately calls the Blow Hose, which will spare Johann from forced fucking. Johann swears it isn't painful.

I never heard from Cosmos again. I supposed he'd learned enough about American women.

Deb wrote her dissertation on the emotionally crippling effects of impotence on married men. She graduated with honors.

I dashed home to Brooklyn around 7:00 P.M. I boiled absurd amounts of pasta for dinner. Otis hadn't played cigarette-pack hockey for days, and she'd pulled all the books off the shelves. Santina had been feeding her Cheese Bits, which she loathes. I spooned out two cans of Chicken of the Sea, and she shut up. I showered. I put on a Putumayo dress. It was pink, and not terribly sexy, but I remembered Belle telling me once that men liked femininity more than tartiness. I didn't agree at the time, but anything was worth a try. I fluffed my hair and sprayed on perfume. I almost went to ask Santina to put makeup on me, but I didn't feel up to a lecture. At 8:10 Alex buzzed.

I opened the door for him. He clutched a bottle of Beaujolais Nouveau in his good hand. In his sling rested a few dozen tulips. He smiled, showing his teeth. "Wanda, you look so . . . feminine," he said. He looked nice in a blue pin-striped oxford and black 501s.

"You say that like a dirty word." I was embarrassed. Alex placed the wine on my kitchen table and dropped the tulips on the couch. I handed him the check and the note from the Beatrices. I said, "How's the wing? You'll probably never play polo again."

He read the note. "Things always work out for you, don't they?" he asked.

I said, "We'll see."

We talked about what had happened the night before. Alex told me he'd tried to call me, but with the drugs he'd barely made it home to crash.

He said, "But we're together now, so it's okay."

"Are we?"

"What do you mean by that?"

"We haven't been getting along so well lately."

"Things have changed."

"Do you mean that your feelings have changed, that our relationship has changed, or that—"

He told me to shut up. He walked me to the couch.

We sat down on the tulips and kissed. It was a nice kiss. Soft and wet, with just the lips.

I asked, "What about your girlfriend?"

He said softly, "I told you a hundred times—I don't have a girlfriend." He drew a line on my jaw with his finger.

"I have a nasty habit of not taking my lovers too seriously," I whispered.

"I'm different from those guys," he said.

We kissed some more. The pasta was boiling over, so I got up and turned it off. I sat back down on the couch with Alex, careful not to bump his shoulder. He kissed me. We spent the night in bed. But that's another story.